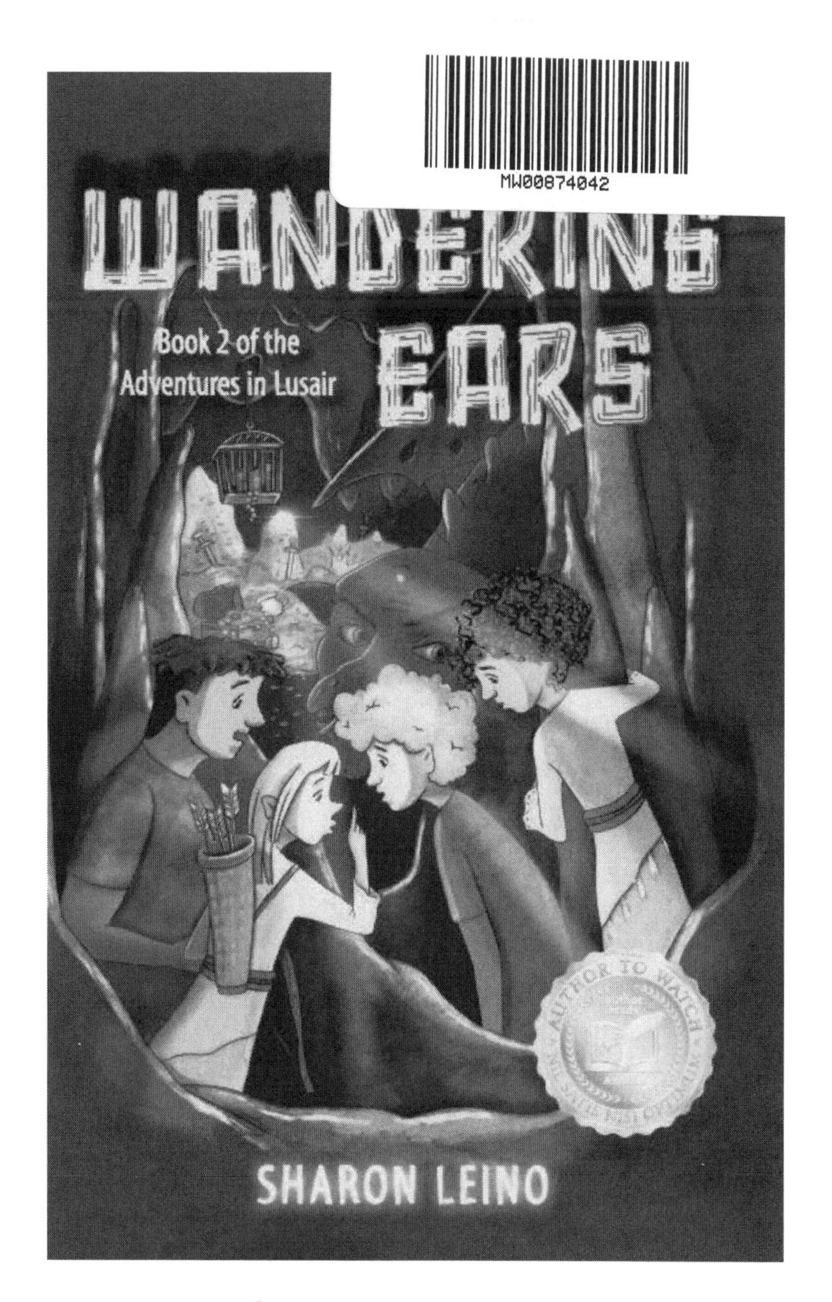

Flint Hills Publishing

Wandering Ears
Book 2 of the Adventures in Lusair

www.sharonleinoauthor.com

Cover & Character Art by Effie Gyf
www.effiegyf.etsy.com.

Cover Design by Amy Albright

Flint Hills Publishing
Topeka, Kansas
www.flinthillspublishing.com

Paperback ISBN 978-1-953583-50-5
Ebook ISBN 978-1-953583-51-2

Library of Congress Control Number 2022917003

Printed in the U.S.A

CONTENTS

CHAPTER 1

"Josephine, stop!" Coach yelled. But Josephine couldn't stop tumbling, over and over. Vaguely she heard yelps of surprise and laughter. Slamming into a wall of classmates, she finally stopped. Her friend, Rudy, was laughing so hard he had to wrap his arms around his stomach. The other classmates looked like a chess set whose pieces were jumbled all over a chess board.

A huge shadow fell over her collapsed form. Coach demanded, "When are you going to listen, Josephine?"

Anticipating her punishment, Josephine jumped to her feet. Black curls bobbing and long legs firing, she ran toward the locker room, calling over her shoulder, "Accidents do happen, ya know!"

English class wasn't much better. Mrs. Kratt was a nightmare, yet Josey completed her assignment before anyone else. With time to ruminate at her desk, she replayed the gym scene in her head.

"Josey," Rudy turned behind with a whisper. "Are you done already? What's a verb? I don't get it."

"Rudy," Josey groaned, "we're not on verbs…"

A foghorn voice boomed, "Josephine, come here and bring your work with you."

She slipped out from the desk and walked at a turtle's pace past Rudy. Would grownups ever get used to calling her Josey instead of Josephine? Ever so slowly she handed over her paper and waited while Mrs. Kratt scanned her work. "I knew you didn't listen. You will do this assignment over and underline all the verbs, not contractions!"

Finally, school was over—what a day of screwups. Slamming her locker door and running ahead of everyone, she left her peers behind. *People don't appreciate that I can think ahead and act quickly*, Josephine reflected on her swift journey home. *There are other people that don't do things right and they don't get yelled or laughed at.*

"Hey, Mom, I'm home!" Josey said, closing the door behind her.

"Come in the kitchen, I want to talk to you." Leaning against the sink with both hands wrapped around her coffee mug, Mother stood quietly. Josey knew that was not a good sign. Rarely did her mother stand quietly with coffee. Usually she drank it quickly, while talking about one thing or the other.

"When are you going to learn that you don't know how to do everything? Or should I ask—when you are going to learn to listen?"

"Who, me?"

Her mother looked around the room and sighed. "Do you see anyone else?"

"Coach called, didn't he. Just because I said I knew how to do a flip and messed up is no reason to call you. Last week Rudy threw a soccer ball and it hit Billy and gave him a black eye and he didn't even get yelled at." Twirling a black curl around her finger, she said, "I flipped into the other line of kids standing across from me. I couldn't help it!" A smile lit up her face, "You know how dominos fall. Well, everyone fell. No one got hurt. Besides, everyone was laughing. Well —almost everyone."

Rolling her eyes, Mother said, "No, this time it was your English teacher. It seems that you don't listen to her instructions either. You complete assignments before she finishes giving the directions. She also said that you won't ask for help, that you pretend you know how to do everything. And THAT is why you do not know proper grammar."

"I do too! She's such a dork! Everyone falls asleep when she's explaining. . ."

"Stop right there! If you know grammar so well, why you are getting Fs on all your papers?"

Without thinking, Josey blurted out, "I'm not a child! Why can't you old . . ." In a quieter voice Josey finished, "Ah, um, grownups, see that?" Her dark brown eyes blinked rapidly, and her small nose twitched like a cornered squirrel. Aware that her mother was studying her, she asked, "What?"

Slowly, words echoed loudly in her ears. "Apparently you know it all. I think you should go to your room."

"I'm sorry, Mom. I'll try. . ."

"Go," Mother snapped.

Pushing herself out of the chair and muttering under her breath softly, Josey headed toward her bedroom, "Sheesh. If it's not Mom, it's Mrs. Kratt, or the Coach." Still grumbling, she entered her bedroom and slammed the door. A tapping at the window drew her attention; she saw red spiked hair and blue eyes, and lots of white teeth grinning at her.

Josey stomped over to the window and raised it. "What do you want, Rudy?"

"Come on. Climb out."

"Can't. I've been sent to my room."

"Come on, just for a little while. You know I hate going home to an empty house," Rudy pleaded.

Josey thought to herself, *Mom wouldn't want him going to an empty house.* His mom and dad had to work late many nights. Usually, they asked if he could stay and eat at her house. *Hmm, they must have forgotten to call. I'm sure Mom won't be too mad. I won't leave the yard and I'll stay near the window so I can hear her call me.*

Climbing out of the window, Josey's shoelace got caught on the window lock. Dangling, leaving her half-in and half-out the window she called, "Rudy, I'm stuck."

Rudy grabbed her foot and pulled; Josey fell on top of him, and they tumbled backwards into the bushes. Untangling themselves, Josey shook her head. She didn't believe what she was seeing.

Rudy jumped up so fast that he knocked Josey down again, then ran over to his newly-appeared friend. "Josey, this is the Knight of Light."

Josey rubbed her eyes and blinked several times. Walking over to the horse and pushing Rudy aside she thought, *What's wrong with him? He didn't have to knock me down. Who is that guy in the light?* Rubbing her eyes once more, she saw in front of her a huge circle of light encompassing a knight on a horse. The shiny brilliance of his armor made her eyes water. Josey approached the horse's muzzle and felt her black curls flutter as the horse snorted. She looked up at the knight, his eyes radiating kindness and trust. She immediately liked him.

Just as Josey started to introduce herself, the knight gestured toward Rudy. In a state of mild disbelief, Josey watched as the knight unveiled a key nearly the size of a football. It was attached to a well-worn chain that he used to drape over Rudy's neck.

"Rudy, I need you to go to Lusair and help a new questor who lost his key. He is fighting an old evil and will need not only this key, but your and Josey's help. Now go!"

Rudy grabbed Josey's hand and dragged her kicking and screaming into the circle of light.

"Are you crazy? Where are we going!" Her voice trailed off as she watched the key around Rudy's neck shrink to a normal size.

They were transported into a beautiful garden with tall bushes all around. There were fountains of water gently spraying in the air and into pools. The soft wind carried a mist from the fountains to the circle of flowers that spread in shifting shades of yellow, blue, and red around the lush green forest. Suddenly the surrounding bushes started to move and encircle Josey and Rudy. The bushes jostled them back and forth like a springboard from bush to bush.

"Hey, stop that! Rudy, what did you drag me into?" Josey cried.

"We have to get out of these bushes. They're starting to grow thorns, and I think they're getting bigger! Ouch!" yelled Rudy.

The bushes circled in so close that they could see the thorns grow. The circle kept shrinking and shrinking and the thorns kept getting closer and closer. It looked like they were going to become pin cushions soon.

Suddenly, a command reverberated, “Stop.”

The bushes parted to free Rudy and Josey just in the nick of time before they became thorny porcupines.

A small girl with silver hair and green almond-shaped eyes glared at them. She held a bow and arrow in a relaxed but cautious grip. “Who are you and how did you get here?”

Josey was still most concerned about the bushes and kept watching them to make sure they weren’t moving. “Why did those bushes attack us? Why did they grow thorns? Who are you?”

“I am Matina, Princess of the Elmorts. Those bushes are called Bushwhackers, and anyone that enters the palace ground unallowed is held by them until someone arrives. It’s a good thing you are innocent, otherwise the thorns would have come out a lot sooner. Now, again—who are you?”

“Are we in Lusair?” Rudy asked.

“Yes. Mortals such as yourself rarely come. In fact, I haven’t seen a human in thousands of years.” Matina’s voice softened and she said, “Well, that is not exactly true. They are here but keep to themselves and we do not bother them. And, I am not allowed off the palace grounds, so I don’t know how many there are.”

At one point in time, mortals like yourself could not bear the power of elven magic, and as a result, they gradually distanced themselves from the elves and us. However, when famine and disease swept through the land, the elves were unjustly accused of causing it and humans demanded their banishment. What the humans failed to realize was that the elves were also suffering from famine and disease.

Rudy couldn't believe it. "Thousands of years? Billy and I were here just last month."

Matina asked, "What is your name and where is this 'Billy?' How did you enter Lusair?"

"The Knight of Light opened a window of time for us. We helped Nipron defeat the Demon of Chaos…"

Rudy didn't have time to finish before Matina put her bow away and ran over to grab his hands.

"It really is you, Rudy. I thought as much when I saw your red hair, but I had to be sure. There are songs and stories written about your and Billy's bravery."

Josey stared at him with eyes as big as headlights. "You've been here before? Is that why you're not afraid of your shadow anymore?"

"Josey, I've told you a million times, but you don't listen. You just blow me off every time I try to talk about it. Remember the time when you wanted to try out for a part in the school play? You were good. I tried to tell you to have faith in yourself. I learned that in Lusair, and you didn't listen or hear a word I said."

She vaguely remembered not even trying out for the part.

She couldn't believe it. Here they were in a different world and all Rudy could talk about was that stupid play. Her mind was spinning as she plunked down on a nearby bench and looked around. Where did this bench come from? Where did this forest come from? She was in a beautiful garden and her neighborhood was gone. No Mom, no houses, no kids playing, no bikes, no one playing ball. Looking at her feet she saw the tall grass that looked like thin tiny feathers. "Am I dreaming?"

"No, Josey, this is real," said Rudy.

Matina sat next to Josey. "Why don't you listen to what others are telling you?" Matina asked.

Josey's brown eyes flashed with anger. "I do, I mean, I don't! I do! I just don't need help all the time. Everyone makes mistakes. Besides, I do ask for help occasionally. Hey, how do you know that I don't listen? What are you, a mind reader?" asked Josey.

"I have the ability to see another's thoughts, but this shows on your face. You have many thoughts tumbling around you, and you just haphazardly choose one and jump into action without thinking it through."

Feeling uncomfortable, Josey changed the subject, "Why don't mortals come here?"

"They don't understand our magic."

"Magic in our world is just a bunch of tricks," Josey chuckled. "Is Lusair a tricky world?"

Matina stood and glared down at Josey. "That's what I mean. Mortals make fun of what they don't understand. In Lusair, magic is real. There came a time when mortals such as yourself could no longer stand the elfin magic and they drifted apart from us. Lies and whispers of lies began when the winds of change brought famine and disease. Elves were blamed and mortals wanted them banished. What they did not know was that elves were dying from famine and disease just as they were."

Rudy asked, "Why didn't they just let the people know that they were suffering too?"

Brushing her silver hair out of her eyes, she was quiet for a long moment. "Because the elves were proud and arrogant and did not want to appear weak to anyone or anything. Grandmother said their arrogance was responsible for the humans not understanding. Not all the mortals left for other worlds—many stayed but don't mingle with the elves anymore. There has been distrust between the elves and the elmorts and the humans ever since."

Josey asked, "So what are elmorts? You said you were an elmort, but you look human like me."

Matina took a deep breath and said, "No, I am not human. We were created just before large numbers of humans left our realm. Powerful elves did not want to see the humans leave. They took the best qualities of the humans and the best qualities of the elves and created elmorts.

"The elmorts had powerful gifts and magic, but our appearance is more human than elfin; because of that we were shunned by the elves. Most of the elves did not welcome us and threw us out of their kingdoms. We had to find our own areas to live and now have larger kingdoms and are more powerful than the elves. Yet they still shun us. Grandmother says it is their great loss."

Before Matina could explain further, the sky turned black, and a howling wind blew with an icy rage. Willow trees swayed frantically as leaves were stripped from their branches. The bushes were crushed under the wind while hundreds of flowers flew past them like specks of dust in a whirlwind. Josey and Matina were blown off the bench onto their backs. Matina's silver hair whipped straight up in the air and swirled around like a merry-go-round out of control.

"We must get back to the palace!" cried Matina.

Matina pulled Josey to her knees, "Don't try to stand," she yelled. "Crawl!"

Josey ignored Matina and tried to stand up. She spread her arms straight out like a scarecrow and bent forward into the wind, but suddenly found herself rolling backwards.

Matina and Rudy crawled over and helped her up onto her knees. Matina yelled, "Crawl, don't walk."

Helpless, Josey crawled between them. They were like snails trying to race for cover as they grabbed tufts of grass to pull them forward. It was difficult to see because the air was filled with hundreds of leaves and flowers swirling around them. Josey bumped into something hard—one of the giant trees in the palace garden. Matina crawled close to her and waved a hand toward a door hidden at the base of the tree.

"Come on," Matina cried as she held the door open.

Rudy jumped through, exclaiming, "Come on, Josey!"

Gasping for breath, Josey looked inside and saw black, nothing but black. Where was Rudy? She was about to ask when Matina pushed her into the hole.

"Hey! There could be an animal inside this tree!" Josey yelled as she tumbled through.

Quickly Matina dropped down beside them, snagging the door behind her shut as she also fell through. It was pitch black until she brought out a tiny globe of light.

"Your actions show the truth. First you stand when you're supposed to crawl, and then you argue about safety," Matina snapped.

"That's not true. I just thought if I angled my body right, I would be able to walk in the wind. And what about an animal, there could've been one in here."

Matina's eye's flashed with anger, "Josey, think! That's your problem, you don't think or listen! The wind blew so hard it stripped leaves off the trees. No one could walk in it. And as far as entering the door, Rudy was already in the tree. I wouldn't have brought you here if it was dangerous."

Josey sat and folded her arms around her knees. "I do think. I wonder about things all the time. A tree with a door? Where's my house? Can we go home now?"

The tree creaked and groaned. It sounded like the wind was trying to pull it out by its roots.

Realizing that the storm was getting stronger, Rudy asked, "Are we in a tornado?"

With shaking hands, Matina placed the bright globe on the ground between them. "I don't know. we've never had a black wind. Nothing like this has ever happened in Lusair."

They listened to the frenzied wind getting louder and louder. "I wonder if Grandmother's right? She's been warning everyone that something bad was about to happen."

"Bad? Like what kind of bad?" asked Rudy.

Matina's large green eyes locked with Josey's. "I don't know. Bad like evil."

Gulping, Josey's words came out in a squeak. "Evil? Like what kind of evil?"

Before she had a chance to answer, they heard a loud roar and shivered as a blanket of fear wrapped around them. Suddenly the wind stopped, and light streamed in under the door. Silence hung in the air and the fear left.

"Did you feel that—fear?" Josey whimpered.

"Yes," Matina whispered.

Rudy crawled to the door and cracked it open and then climbed out. "I don't know why you're whispering. We're safe now."

Matina climbed out. "Look! Everything is just as it was. The leaves are still on the trees. The bushes are tall and standing guard and the grass and flowers are standing straight. Not a stem is broken."

Josey was last to leave the safety of the tree and couldn't believe it. "I know all the leaves were stripped off this tree. I saw it. And those bushes were crushed."

Matina ran. "Come, follow me."

Running, they could see the palace appear, bit by bit. Most of it was hidden behind thick foliage. Steps jutted from the underbrush. Towers and walls appeared here and there in a tangle of vines like a jigsaw puzzle. Running toward the palace that was hidden by trees and bushes, they were awed by what they saw, as little by little, the palace's beauty was revealed.

"Wow, a real palace," Rudy breathed.

"Where is everyone?" Josey asked.

"I don't know. Something is wrong—it has never been this quiet and the guards are gone. Maybe they're in the great hall. Let's go there."

Hundreds of lit torches reflected onto woven tapestries hanging on the walls. Josey and Rudy stared in awe at the different scenes that came to life: battles, celebrations with kings and heroes—all moving and urging them on. They came to a great room with a large domed ceiling built of clear glass. Clouds raced overhead, taunting.

The great hall was empty.

As was the throne.

CHAPTER 2

"Quickly! We must go to Grandmother," Matina exclaimed as she ran into a small room across from the throne. Josey and Dexter followed close behind as they made their way up a stairway. Stepping out of the stairway, they came to a hallway with large sconces holding flaming torches. It was eerily quiet—even their footsteps were quiet. A massive door that reached from the floor to the ceiling appeared at the end of the hallway.

Matina waved her hand and the door opened quietly. "Wait here! I will call you."

Josey stopped in her tracks. "How could she open a huge door with just a flick of the wrist? Rudy, have you ever seen a door this big? I wonder if they have giants living here?"

Edging slowly into the archway, Josey continued, "Why do we have to wait here so long? It won't hurt if we peek in."

"Josey, we're not supposed to go in yet. Matina didn't ask us, but *ordered* us to wait," Rudy whispered.

Josey couldn't stand still. Her toes kept inching into the room. Sunlight flooded through large windows that had delicate birds and flowers carved into their frames. Heavy vines grew from an enormous wooden headboard that was thick and had strange words carved into it. The floor was filled with plants and flowers that grew out of the floor with paths circling around the bed and to the windows. Smells of lavender and honeysuckle filled the room, tickling Josey's nose. Numerous sheer curtains knotted at the ceiling, gently draped around a bed.

Josey stopped abruptly, feeling as though she had walked into a freezer. Cold. So cold, she couldn't move or talk. Something tickled her brain and she managed to cry out. Rudy stood in the doorway with his mouth open, his red hair standing straight up.

Matina pulled the curtains back, "Grandmother! Stop! Don't frighten my friends."

Josey felt the cold slip away, "What happened?"

Matina's cheeks were red with embarrassment. "I'm sorry. It was rude of my grandmother to investigate your memories without asking permission." Matina's voice changed to a harsh, stern tone when she said, "I did ask you to wait outside."

"Come closer, Josey. Time has been unkind and taken away my sight. Since I'm not able to see, I needed to know very quickly who entered my room uninvited. Much has happened and time is precious. Come closer and take my hand," said Grandmother.

Josey was surprised to see an old, but beautiful looking woman. She had long white hair and only a few wrinkles. She looked frail lying there. Josey felt warmth flowing through her body while she held Grandmothers' hand.

"Rudy, please come and let me hold your hand for a moment."

Rudy approached the bed slowly and put his hand in hers. He felt trust and purpose flowing through his spirit.

"You both have been sent here by the Knight of Light to help Matina find her mother and destroy the evil that has fallen upon us."

"Mother is missing?" Matina asked.

Without notice, a tall stern woman stepped from behind the headboard. A black helmet shadowed her face, but eyes blazed like lighthouse beams. Josey gasped. She had never seen anyone so fierce looking.

"Sulee, what are you doing here?" Matina asked. "Where is Mother? Where are Grandmother's servants? Why is a warrior and not a servant with Grandmother?"

"Matina, as I said before, your mother has been stolen away. Everyone has gone to find her except Sulee, who stayed behind to guard us."

"How? Why?"

Sulee explained in short, clipped tones. "We were gathered in the Great Hall. The air became black. The wind blew with a roar. Your mother vanished."

Matina's spine stiffened and her voice wavered, "How will they find her? Do they know where to look?"

Sulee shook her head no, but Grandmother hissed, "Matina, you and your friends must find the questor…"

"It has been decided," the warrior interrupted. "Until your mother returns, you are not to leave your grandmother's side. I have been left behind to make sure you both are safe."

"Sulee, you are not in charge. I alone make the decisions until my daughter is found!"

At Grandmother's words, Sulee's eyes flared with anger. Her posture stiffened even more. But Sulee was quiet and bowed her head. "I am truly sorry, your majesty. I am concerned for the safety of you and the princess. It would be tragic if anything happened to either of you."

"Yes, yes," said Grandmother as she waved her hand. "Please, go stand by the door. I need to talk privately with my granddaughter."

“Grandmother…?”

“Hush, child.” She waited till she knew that Sulee could not overhear. In a voice barely above a whisper she said, “Listen closely—I know you two are from another world, but time has a way of giving us what we need, and you must play an important part in this, or you would not be here.

I told everyone bad times would come. Well, come they did. I also told your mother that her advisors were wrong. We should not be isolated and hidden. We should have learned this lesson from the elves long ago. Because of our arrogance we felt evil could not touch us.”

“I remember how everyone laughed and called you senile behind your back, Grandma.”

“Our people thought there was nothing their magic couldn’t control. They have forgotten who gave them the magic. They forgot it was to be used only for good, not for selfish and pompous desires.”

The old woman sank back against the pillows. “You must seek the questor. He can tell you how to find your mother.”

“What’s a questor?” Josey asked.

“A questor has an unending thirst for knowledge—one who cares for Lusair and all those who live in it. His quest to help others is so great that he forgets all else, even sleeping and eating. Because of this he has an assistant who sees to his basic needs. The questor is also the one we go to when there is trouble. He is the one that calls the Knight of Light when needed.”

Rudy asked, "Are you talking about Nipron? I met him the last time I was here."

Surprised, Grandmother asked Rudy how he came to know Nipron. Rudy told her how he and his friend Billy were in Lusair a month ago.

"We helped Nipron and his assistant Dinky. We defeated an evil wizard who was the tool of the Demon of Chaos. The Knight of Light gave me a key to enter Lusair. We used a lot of light to send the evil wizard back to the demon. It was amazing, the instant the evil wizard was gone, the whole place came alive. Before it was dark and black and the trees were crumbling from rot and snow just kept falling. Then suddenly it was spring, and the grass was there, and the trees were alive and blooming with leaves right before our eyes. It was awesome."

Grandmother was quiet as she considered her words carefully. "Nipron is in the mountains, and no one can find him, but he has trained many other questors to help. Lucas is the questor in charge of our area. He is new and inexperienced. He lost his key to other worlds, like the one you are wearing, Rudy. He has been frantic and calling on everyone to help him find it, which was very unwise."

"Questors are seen as all-knowing and at times to be feared and respected, especially by those with evil intentions," Grandmother continued. "Lucas, on the other hand, appears to be inadequate and not one that is feared or respected. Therefore, it has emboldened others that are sinister to act on their evil quest. Creatures that were banished from this realm are returning. Old magic that was evil is growing stronger."

"Grandmother, how do you know this Lucas so well?"

"We grew up together and our friendship gave us a special bond. He is extremely kind, and has a true heart, but needs to develop a more confident aura. People misinterpret his kindness and humbleness for weakness. He is not weak, but one of the most powerful questors in existence. He is more powerful than even he realizes. He just needs to recognize his power."

Struggling to get a silver ring off her finger, Grandmother handed it to Matina. "Take this and put it on. You need to show this to Lucas, or he will not talk to you. He created it when we were young and told me to put it on if I ever needed his aid. He knew that we would both change in appearance as we got older, but he would recognize the ring as he engraved special flowers on it."

Josey looked at the ring and couldn't believe the tiny flowers that were perfectly engraved. She reached out to touch it, but Matina took it quickly from her grandmother's hand and put it on. A a small circle of light surrounded her hand and the ring.

"Grandmother, what about Josey and Rudy? You know mortals and elmorts aren't on the best of terms."

"There is something special about them. I am not certain what it is, but you must make sure they are with you, always. You cannot find your mother without them, otherwise the Knight of Light would not have sent them."

Josey looked up from the ring to find Matina staring at her. “What did I do now? Did I miss something?”

“Didn’t you hear what Grandmother said?”

Heat rushed to Josey’s face. “I was looking at the ring and didn’t hear you.”

“Josey!” Matina snapped. “You and Rudy are supposed to go with me to find my mother.”

Josey narrowed her eyes and said, “Well, you could be nicer about it!”

Grandmother studied Matina for a long time before she spoke. “You have been sheltered within the palace grounds for many years. The world outside has changed, and the change is not for the better. The people of the land are angry. Not because we caused the evil, but because we did nothing to prevent it. They may direct their anger at you.”

“Can’t be that bad.” Rudy had walked to the window and stood looking out. “Everything here is beautiful and healthy.”

“Here, yes.” Grandmother agreed. “Beyond the palace you will see a difference. There is much destruction of the land. Our magic keeps things abundant inside, but outside our subjects have not fared as well.”

“What do you mean?” Matina asked.

“There is no caring or giving to others—especially to those in need. There are boundaries and gates where none existed before. People are confused about what to believe because their leaders are themselves confused and cannot agree on things that need to be done."

"A quiet evil has invaded the land without a battle. It seeps into lives such that the people are unaware. They only see the destruction of the land and not their thinking."

"What is wrong with their thinking?" Rudy asked.

"The leaders blame the people for wanting too much and the people blame the leaders for their greed and corruption, but nothing changes. Anger invades this land like a festering wound while people go hungry and homeless. Everyone is so busy they do not take time to think about others or how their actions affect others. There isn't even respect for the land or its living creatures—they are being destroyed without thought."

"Matina, you are young to use your gift, but because you are going on a dangerous journey you must use your gift of fire," Grandmother continued. "I know you have not been trained, but I also know that you have been sneaking out of the palace and watching others being trained every day. You also have been practicing in the woods. Don't look so surprised—I know all that goes on around here. I didn't stop you because I've been training you since you were a child to follow instructions and to have self-control. That is why I allowed you to practice; you have great self-control."

"Under normal circumstances I would never ask you to use this power, but you must practice it on your journey. You will encounter monsters and need to learn to control your gift quickly so that it becomes automatic. Start with small things like lighting a small campfire or a torch. Anything more requires great discipline over your powers."

"I'm not going anywhere," Josey whispered to Rudy. "This is too much."

"Hush, and listen," Grandmother insisted. "Stop at the boskers and have Tomtee go with you. His people may not be helpful, but Tomtee is a trusted friend. He has magic that you will need. Now go and pack for your journey, but don't let Sulee know what you are up to."

"What kind of magic?" asked Josey. The queen did not answer but ordered them to go and pack.

As the three were leaving the room, Sulee towered over them and held up her hand for them to stop.

"I expect to dine with you three in a couple hours."

They all nodded and continued out of the room. Hurrying down the stairs to the kitchen, Sulee appeared in front of them at the bottom of the steps. "What are you planning? It is too early to eat."

Rudy shook his head. "How did you get here? We just left you."

Matina quickly sent a thought to her grandmother asking her to call Sulee back to her room. "I thought I would show my friends the kitchen . . ."

Sulee suddenly disappeared.

"Boy, that was close. Where did she go?" asked Josey.

"I sent Grandmother a thought so that she would call Sulee back to her room. Come on, we have to hurry."

They went to the kitchen and found it silent and the fires cold; the cook watched them in silence. She had been ordered not to cook until the queen returned.

They hurried into a side room off from the kitchen that was filled with food and supplies. Dried meat hung on hooks, bins were full of vegetables, fruits, nuts, and beans. They had to duck under long strings of dried mushrooms, red peppers, and onions. The smell of salt, pepper, and spices in tiny open barrels tickled their noses.

"I can't believe all the stuff you can fit in these small sacks," Josey said as they excitedly claimed the food.

Matina handed them more bags. "We may be gone a long time and need to take enough food to get by. Grab some of those meat bones and wrap them up. Take the dried mushrooms and onions hanging in the corner, we can use water to hydrate them later. Rudy, scoop those beans and rice into those bags hanging next to them and make sure you tie the bags tight."

After the sacks were full and packed, they hurried out of the room.

"Come on, we must go to the weapon room next," Matina instructed.

"That sounds great," Rudy shouted. "What kind are we going to use?"

Matina opened another door with a wave of her hand. There were crossbows hanging on the wall with quivers full of arrows next to them. Shields and swords were stacked next to each other. There was a display filled with knives of every sort and size. Matina started tucking knives in her boots, belt, and waist holder. She then selected bows and arrows. Rudy and Josey stared as she hurriedly packed her weapons.

"Why are you just standing there?" Matina asked.

"You mean you want us to pick out weapons too?" replied Rudy in bewilderment.

"Yes and get busy—we don't have much time before we are to meet Sulee for dinner."

Rudy went straight away to the knives and began to examine them when Josey reminded him that he had never been in a knife fight.

"Why don't you pick out a bow and arrows? At least we know how to use them from gym class last semester."

Reluctantly, Rudy put the knives back and chose a bow but added a sword. "I can't resist, Josey—this may come in handy."

Josey rolled her eyes and finished packing. They hid the weapons and food pack sacks under the beds in their nearby guest rooms and went to have dinner with Sulee.

Dinner was sparse because the cook was ordered not to use the fires. Fresh tomatoes and baby carrots, along with lush lettuce, radishes, peas, and cheese was their banquet. After eating with somber conversation, they said good night, leaving Grandmother and Sulee to finish their tea.

Lying in bed, Josey couldn't help thinking about their journey into Lusair, let alone how she was going to get home. Tossing and turning, she fell into a restless sleep. She woke to Matina's whisper in her ear, "Get dressed, quickly. It's time to leave."

Josey pulled a blue tunic over her head and wondered why Matina wouldn't let her wear her own clothes. Tights and a tunic were not her idea of traveling clothes.

Hmpf, I'm not giving up my gym shoes, Josey thought as she finished tying her shoelaces.

Josey looked up as Matina lifted her backpack, slipped her arms into the straps, then adjusted it to fit comfortably on her back. She helped Josey do the same and then told her to follow.

Just outside their rooms, Matina motioned Josey to stop and be quiet. Sulee was sitting asleep outside of Rudy's room. Josey let out a gasp and was ready to say something when Matina put both her hands over Josey's mouth. Her eyes warned Josey to be quiet. They stood quietly, barely breathing as they waited to see if Sulee would wake up. They tiptoed past Sulee and slowly opened the door. Matina woke Rudy, and in hushed whispers told him to get dressed. They waited for him in the hall, watching Sulee slowly breathe in and out. It was taking forever, and Josey was about to open his door again when finally, Rudy came out.

When they had walked further away from Sulee, Matina hissed, “Where are the clothes I laid out for you?”

Whispering, he said, “I am not wearing tights, these jeans are just fine!”

They hurried away from where Sulee was still sleeping and entered the palace courtyard.

On the wall were three unlit torches in holders—they each took one. Matina arched one of her hands and wove it quickly back and forth then pointed one finger toward the torches, gently trying to throw fire. A loud swoosh and the torches blazed brightly.

“I actually did it.”

Rudy looked at his torch and said, “Maybe a lighter touch would do next time. Just so we don’t burn down the palace.”

Scowling, Matina knew he was right and turned to follow a sandy, worn path through a dark forest. A slight breeze rustled through the pines as they whispered softly to one another, telling secrets of long ago.

Not wanting to disturb the stillness surrounding them, Josey whispered, “Do you have a map to find the questor?”

“Not exactly. Grandmother gave me the impression from her mind. I know the way, and it will take us until tomorrow to reach Tomtee.”

Josey frowned, “I'm sure my mother will worry if I’m gone too long. I wish I could let her know I’m okay."

"Don't worry," Matina said. "Remember time is different here. A day in Lusair is less than a second in your world. Even if you stayed here a year, you could return within hours of the time you left. Your mother would never know you were gone."

Beyond the Elmort palace grounds, the darkened forest looked menacing, with frightful sounds bouncing all around them. The trees were no longer tall and straight but jagged and bent. The branches appeared weighed down by something that reminded Josey of despair.

Rudy asked, "Are we gonna walk all night? I'm hungry."

"We'll be in Mort's Glen soon." Matina said. "There's a journey house there that's hidden by spells. It is a rest stop where elmorts stay to sleep and become refreshed when traveling."

"Wish I had spells that would hide the mess in my room. Why did we have to leave in the middle of the night, anyway?" asked Josey.

"Didn't you hear Sulee? She was left behind to make sure that Grandma and I were protected. She would never have let us leave."

"She must be a sound sleeper not to hear us leave the palace. And why was she sleeping outside my door?" Rudy asked.

Matina continued to lead them through the forest. "Sulee refused to sleep through the night and was determined to stand guard outside your door, Rudy. She knew of your adventures with Nipron and thought you would encourage us to leave. Fortunately, Grandmother gave me some sleeping powder that would make Sulee sleep. She used to have trouble sleeping—she would use the root of the Valerian plant that grows in her room and grind it down to a powder. When Sulee wasn't watching, I put it in her tea."

"Remind me not to drink tea with your grandmother!" Rudy squawked.

CHAPTER 3

They continued walking when a mournful cry filled the air and stopped them dead in their tracks. Again, the cry shattered the silence with the appearance of a trio: an elmort, an elf, and a mortal chained together, walking slowly as the heavy chain that bound them together weighed them down. Their eyes filled with tears, and sorrow etched their faces, as they warned of evil in Lusair, chanting as one, "To all who will listen! Lusair is in trouble because no one will govern. All go about doing what they want when they want. Greed and lust for power have taken over."

They repeated the same mantra over and over, uttering prolonged heart-rending cries in-between.

Matina quickly stepped off the path and told Rudy and Josey to do the same. They watched in silence as the three walked past them without so much as looking in their direction.

“Why are they chained like that and crying out so dreadfully?” Rudy wondered aloud.

“They are called criers—they come out in time of sorrow and destruction. Grandmother told me they are rare. They are weighed down by chains of despair and sadness. They only come out when evil reigns in Lusair,” Matina answered.

Even as the criers disappeared along the path, the mournful sound of their mantra still rang in the party’s ears.

After a few hours walking, Matina, Josey, and Rudy stepped out of the woods. Moonlight filtered down onto a grassy knoll.

“Here we are,” Matina said. “Mort’s Glen.”

Josey and Rudy struggled to see, but kept walking, straining their eyes until instantaneously they were in a house filled with light.

“How’d you do that?” Josey’s eyes were large as Matina’s shield, filled with surprise.

Matina’s voice tinkled in laughter. "I told you it was hidden. Weren’t you listening, Josey?”

“Of course, I was. But I didn’t know you meant invisible. I thought I could see it because we were together.”

Matina ducked her head, “I’m sorry. You know you haven’t been listening very well.”

In silence they took off their backpacks and placed them on three beds laid out side by side.

Josey looked around and said, “Wow, even *my* room doesn’t have dust balls this big. I gotta get rid of those spider webs hanging over the beds.”

Rudy laughed. “Is this where the three bears lived?” The girls looked at him puzzled. “Get it? There’re three beds in a row!”

Matina ignored the comment and wandered through the house. “This place is supposed to be spotless. Something’s wrong!”

“It’s not that bad,” Josey said thinking of her own messy room where books, shoes, and clothes were strewn everywhere. They all followed Matina into the dusty living room.

She waved her hands in the air. “Look at the dust balls. There’s no food prepared, and look, there’s no fire in the fireplace.” Angrily, she waved her hand at the fireplace. *Swoosh*—an explosion of wind produced a huge roaring fire. They all three stared with their mouths open.

“Do you think it’s going to burn like that all night? If so, it may burn the place down,” Rudy said.

Matina walked to the fireplace and stood near the fire, slowly moving her hand down. As she gestured, the fire burned lower and lower. She thought it was a good thing she had snuck out of the palace to watch how others were trained to control fire. She just didn't realize that she had that much power. She reviewed in her mind what she had seen in the training sessions. The most important thing was to control one's own emotions. She knew she was very good at that and realized the games she used to play with her grandmother had taught her well—except when she lost her temper.

I need to control my temper better, Matina thought to herself. Josey and Rudy stood staring at the fire and then at Matina.

"I better get to those cobwebs and clean them away if we are going to get any sleep tonight," Josey spoke. "I can't stand spiders and don't want one hanging over my bed." She saw a broom next to the fireplace in the corner and took it to the bedroom.

Rudy went to see what was in the kitchen. Looking in the cupboards, he asked, "Not much here except some cheese and bread. Want some?"

"No," chorused both girls. So Rudy ate all the cheese.

"I think we should sleep with our clothes on—we only have a few hours to rest," Matina said as she settled on her bed. "Maybe the evil of the land has bled the magic away from the house?"

Josey finished cleaning the cobwebs and put the broom away, then climbed in her own bed. "It could be." She punched her pillow and wondered in the quiet of the night what Rudy had gotten her into.

Finally, Rudy came in munching on some cheese and bread, and stretched out on his bed. “Hopefully the magic will give us better food in the morning.”

Brushing her hands through her black curls, Josey said, “I’m tired.” Thoughts of the strange world swirled in her mind, but she fell asleep before she could make any sense of it.

~ ~ ~

Moans and groans from the kitchen woke Josey. She jumped out of bed and ran to see what was happening. She watched Matina’s green almond eyes flash with anger as she was slamming cupboard doors.

“What’s the matter? What are you looking for?” Josey stepped hesitantly through the doorway.

Matina pointed at the table. “We only have tea and toast for breakfast.”

Groaning with a shake of her head, Josey stomped back to the bedroom. “Is that what all the moaning is about?” She put her gym shoes on and yelled, “Get a grip will ya, we have food in the sacks.”

“I know that, but there was supposed to be a nice breakfast already prepared for us. I don’t want to start our trip by having to prepare food.”

Josey muttered, “Let’s eat what’s here, it’s not your last meal you know.”

They quickly ate the sparse breakfast and left the Journey House. Josey looked back at the weather-beaten house that needed painting, and the neglected yard filling with weeds. She wondered if the magic wasn't dying.

Rounding a bend, they came upon a small group of people walking slowly, one foot shuffling in front of the other. Threadbare and colorless clothes draped their thin bodies. They didn't look up, but stared at the ground as they walked.

Matina laid her hand on the arm of one of the elderly women. With a startled cry, the woman pulled her arm away. Another of their group pushed Matina away as they surrounded the old woman in a protective circle.

"I'm sorry. I didn't mean to frighten you. Is there anything I can do to help?" Matina asked.

Without answering, they scurried into the woods and hid behind a clump of trees.

"Please, let me help you," Matina called.

"Why should you want to help us?" the old woman's voice crackled. "Go on your way and leave us be."

Matina dug into her pack. "Here, we have some food. You're welcome to it."

"How much do you want for it?" the old woman asked.

Matina looked shocked. She glanced at Josey in dismay.

"Nothing. It's free," Josey shouted. She turned to Matina. "It is free, isn't it? They don't look like they have any money."

"Of course."

Hushed whispers broke out among the group. Josey could see they were hungry but were afraid to accept the food.

Rudy shook his head and said, "Josey, they think it's poison or spoiled. Let's eat some to prove it's not."

Rudy and Josey took small bites from the bread, cheese, and fruits. Then Matina placed the remainder on the side of the road.

A small girl ran to Josey with her thin hand stretched out. Josey handed her the grapes that she had been tasting. Eagerly, the little girl grabbed them and ran back to the group. Josey watched as the little girl gave it to the elderly woman, who in turn gave each person one grape at a time.

Matina once again begged the people to come and eat but they did not leave their area of safety.

Rudy and Josey emptied all the food from their pack and said, "Come on, Matina, let's leave the food. Maybe they'll come and get it after we leave."

After only a few steps, they heard the small group yell, "Thank you." Josey watched them patiently wait while the elderly woman distributed the food. She couldn't help but wonder why the people didn't trust them.

Matina remembered what Grandmother had told them about the poor and lack of trust in their world. *No wonder they don't trust us. They are starving. How could Mother allow this to happen?* she thought.

Questions swirled in Josey's mind. *Are there people that are poor in my world?* As they continued walking, she realized that she had never met a poor person before. *Yeah, I've seen them on television programs, but they always got help. Didn't they? Guess I'll have to ask Mom about it when I get back.*

Rudy interrupted everyone's thoughts. "How far are the boskers?"

"They're just over this next hill," said Matina. When they got there, she gasped.

A mile of fallen trees were strewn in haphazard piles across the gouged land. Rains had cut deep scars into the earth. A jagged barricade ran along the destroyed land as far as the eye could see. Boskers were busy cutting and piling wood while others were hauling dirt and filling the deep scars in the land.

"Gee, don't they know anything about erosion?" Rudy asked. "Even I know that if you cut everything down the land will erode the soil, especially on these hills."

"Of course, they do! The boskers have cared for forests for hundreds of years," Matina yelled. "The forest is their home. Who could have done this to them?" Matina ran down the hill along the fence toward a gate. "We have to find Tomtee."

Josey hurried after her and watched the people on the opposite side of the gate. They glared at the small group with anger and distrust on their faces. Their black coiled hair tied on top of their heads emphasized the golden hue of their skin. Large coal black eyes followed every step with suspicion at their approach. They kept their arms folded, and frowns deepened. They made no attempt to open the gate to welcome them.

A young, bearded man atop the gate held his arm out and flexed his hand as the party approached. It was a signal to stop. He climbed over the gate, walked toward them, and bowed. Slowly he extended his arms and he and Matina embraced.

“Tomtee, what’s going on?”

He bowed once again. “I’m sorry, Matina, but the boskers will not welcome you here. You are allowed to pass through, but you cannot stay.”

Her green eyes pooled with tears, “But why? The boskers have been our friends for centuries.”

“They do not blame your people for the evil that has come upon the land, but they are angry for your lack of help. The evil of greed began last year. We allowed the furlets to come in and glean the leftover timber after we harvested the forest. This year the furlets were not satisfied with what we had cut. Without permission they did this.” Tomtee waved his arm at the destruction. What had once been a forest of lush trees whose branches beautifully intertwined, was gone.

“The furlets are no longer welcomed in our land. No one is. Your people were to govern. They have not done so in a long time. They refuse to hear our complaints. They do not hear anyone’s complaints anymore. The elmorts no longer are welcome here.”

"What are furlets?" asked Josey.

Tomtee looked at Josey as though she were an insect ready to be squashed. The very mention of a furlet made anger surge through his body like an electrical storm. He managed to speak in a voice that was harsh and low. "They are small beings covered with fur that have a pig's face but feet and hands of a human. They usually steal anything and everything with the excuse that they just borrowed it. They pretend to be nice and honor your ways, but they never tell the whole truth. They are a nuisance that we have put up with for years because they helped free us all from the evil wizard. This is the last straw; we will not allow them anywhere near us again."

Matina's voice broke as tears spilled from her eyes. "I'm sorry. So sorry, Tomtee. But the furlets, they're so small, they are not even two feet high. They couldn't have slaughtered all these trees. How were they able to do this? It doesn't make sense."

"Of course it doesn't, but when there is no one to use logic and common sense to govern, then the mob rules with emotion and prejudice. It is a mystery—I can hardly believe it myself, but there seems to be no other answer," said Tomtee.

"We elmorts were wrong. Grandmother said we were." Turning, Matina stumbled, "Come on. We'd better go on."

The gate opened to allow them to walk through while the boskers lined each side of the path, forcing the three to walk single file.

Josey followed, “I thought your grandmother said we needed Tomtee to find your mother?”

Tomtee heard what Josey said and ran after them. “What is this about your mother?”

“She’s missing.” The words fell quickly out of Matina’s mouth. “Grandmother told us we had to go to the mountains to find the questor, Lucas, so he could contact the Knight of Light, and that we needed you to come with us and help.”

Tomtee raised his chin and his black hair swung from the top knot of his head. “You certainly can’t go without me. Come on, let’s be on our way.”

~ ~ ~

After walking for a short time, they passed through a part of the bosker’s forest that had not been cut. Josey marveled at the giant trees. Free of brush and undergrowth, the forest seemed to go on forever. Their majesty created a peaceful stillness that made her heart swell. Sun rays were everywhere, and the arbors of lush leaves hovered overhead. But too soon the forest ended, and a wide river greeted them.

“Sure looks muddy for a river,” Rudy said. Going closer, he noticed something in a cage trying to keep its head above the fast-flowing water. Quickly, he ran to the river’s edge and pulled the cage out of the water. “Look, someone put a baby fox in this cage.”

Sitting very still with soaked red fur and large round eyes, it stared at Rudy. Tomtee picked up the cage, ready to throw it back into the water "Aggh, that is no fox! That is a mewling, and you should have left it in the river."

Josey could not believe her ears and grabbed the cage from Tomtee. "What's the matter with you? Can't you see it's just a baby fox."

Tomtee put his hands on his hips and shook his head. "Okay, okay, I was being a bit harsh, but we must be careful with this mewling. It looks like a baby fox now but could change into a baby bird or even a kitten in an instant. Its cry is pitiful, and you feel so badly for it that you want to pick it up and take care of it. The truth is it will steal your magic and you'll be left with nothing."

The little mewling cried a tearful heart-rending cry that tugged at Rudy. He reached out and took the cage from Josey. "Since I don't have any magic, I'll take it out of the cage, and we can let it go on its way." Before anyone could say or do anything, Rudy lifted the baby fox out of the cage and petted it.

"Rudy, don't!" yelled Matina and Tomtee together.

Before they finished yelling, the baby fox turned into a baby bird and grabbed Rudy's key and flew away.

"Hey, bring that back here!" Rudy ran after the baby bird but then it just disappeared. Rudy pulled his red hair and yelled, "What are we going to do without that key?"

No one spoke—the group was paralyzed as though panic had frozen them into living statues.

In a hushed voice Matina said, "Maybe the questor can still help us."

Rudy folded his arms at the waist and bent over, "I think I'm going to throw up."

Josey rushed over and patted him on the back. "Rudy, it'll be okay. I'm sure Tomtee or Matina will think of something."

Tomtee snarled, "Don't count on it."

Matina stiffened her back—she was angry at Tomtee for being so rude. "I am sure the questor will know just what to do. Come on, we've wasted enough time."

Rudy felt as low as a frog in mud and remembered that the knight had said this questor would need their help. *What am I going to do now?* he thought.

Josey said, "I hate to ask, but do we need to cross the river?"

Tomtee was glad that he could solve that problem. He took the wooden cage and broke it into pieces, laying it out in the shape of a rectangle. He then called out his magic and the wood wiggled and squiggled together to form a small raft. Tomtee then placed it in the water. With a blink of his eyes, the raft exploded to a size that would carry all of them across. He kept one piece of wood to make a pole that would guide the raft.

The raft floated along quietly and then began to slowly spin. The spinning continued until they were halfway across, when suddenly the pole was jerked out of Tomtee's hand.

The spinning stopped; the raft froze while they listened to beautiful sounds of life below the river. Musical words filled the air, of water flowing, moving life along, words of love and peaceful yearning to live in the waters below.

“Kelpies!’ yelled Tomtee. He hurriedly pulled small plugs of cork from his pack and told everyone to quickly put them in their ears.

Just as they finished, a man full of seaweed, no, a horse full of seaweed, exploded into view. They were confused by what they saw because the black-green kelpie was shifting its shape between a horse and a man as though it couldn’t make up its mind.

Tomtee and Matina stood together, ready to fight. “Why do you detain us? We travel peacefully,” Tomtee declared.

A warbling voice answered, “You took my fox and now I need to take one of you.”

“I am Matina, Princess of the Elmorts, and I demand that you release us.”

The kelpie became more confused than ever and changed from a man with hooves to a horse with a man’s head, switching back and forth so quickly that they became dizzy just watching him. Tomtee knew from days past that this must be a youngster that couldn’t decide what to do, so he waved his hand and moved the kelpie two miles from them down the river. He then hurriedly caused a wind to push the raft onto the shore.

Taking out their ear plugs, Rudy asked, “What was that thing?”

Josey walked to the water’s edge to see if it was coming back. “Yeah, why did it keep changing shapes?”

“What did it mean we took the fox and it needed to take us?” Rudy asked.

“It was a kelpie that sings to its victims and drags them down under the water to its home,” Tomtee explained. “They usually appear as a man or horse, but we were lucky this was a young one and couldn’t decide what to do. We took his dinner from him, and he wanted one of us to replace it.”

Rudy shook his head as he walked to where Josey was standing. “It doesn’t look like he is coming back.”

“Come on, we need to keep going,” said Matina. They followed her and walked along a worn path until they came to a ledge with rocks strewn everywhere. They looked over the ledge and could see a deep canyon with more rocks.

“Where did all the rocks come from? How could so many be in one spot? Is mining going on here?” Rudy asked.

Tomtee nodded. “Yes, but mining was supposed to have stopped 500 years ago. Just another sign that no one is taking care of Lusair.”

“Guess we should camp at the bottom of that smaller mound below. Wait a minute, Josey. I’ll help you. It’s a bit tricky climbing down,” Tomtee said.

"I am fine and don't need your help," Josey muttered as she worked her way over the rocks. Her foot slipped, and she fell into a deep hole. Air whistled in her ears as she sailed down a slick tunnel into the earth.

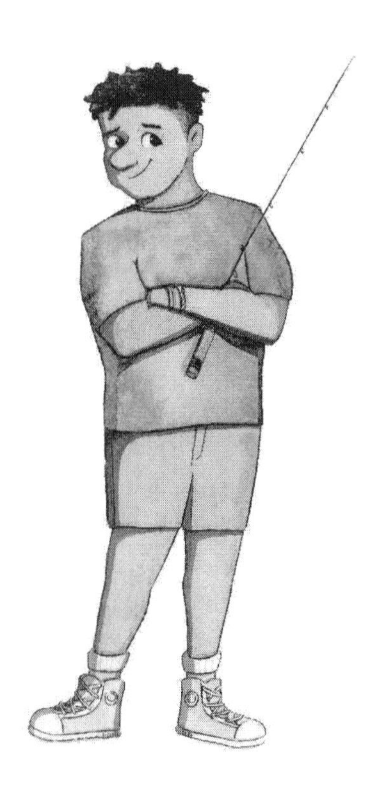

CHAPTER 4

Dumped into a small cave at the bottom of the canyon, Josey staggered to her feet, “Whew, what a ride! I’ve never been on such a fast slide! Maybe I should’ve let Tomtee help me.” She saw light and stumbled toward it. Looking up, she could see everyone at the top calling for her. Cupping her hands to her mouth she shouted, “Here I am!”

Matina heard her and walked to the edge of the canyon. Looking down she saw a tiny speck, but her elfin vision brought Josey into view. “How did you get down there so fast?” Matina yelled back.

Before Josey could answer, Matina, Tomtee, and Rudy were standing beside her. "Yikes! Me? How'd you get here so fast?"

Rudy yelled, "We flew, Josey! We flew!"

"Flying!? All I did was slide through rock."

Grumbling, she led them to the small cave and showed them the tunnel slide. Josey motioned for the others to be quiet, she thought she heard something. A small whining sound came from close by.

Matina walked over to a pile of rocks and lifted them one by one. Underneath lay a small hairy creature covered in mud and bruises. Gently, she placed it on her lap and cleaned off the mud. Josey thought it looked like a baby pig, except it had tiny human hands and large feet—and talk about fur. Its long pointy nose snuffled as Matina brushed off the mud.

"What kind of animal is that?" Josey asked.

Matina took gauze from her leather pouch to wrap its leg. "A furlet is not an animal."

Tomtee pointed at the small being. "A furlet is just what you see. Thieves and butchers of forests! Matina, why are you healing that furlet anyway?"

"He's hurt! Besides, think about it! How can something this small destroy so much of your forests? There would have to be thousands of them, and you know that there are only a couple hundred alive on Lusair."

Rudy looked at Tomtee in disbelief. "How could they chop even one tree? They're not even two feet tall and look at his skinny arms. There are no muscles. They're so small it would take them a year to chop one tree."

Josey gently touched the furlet's head. "Are they all this tiny?"

Tiny beady eyes opened. "Oh, honored princess, healer of all things great and small! I am your servant forever."

Matina patted the furlet's head and sat him up. "You can thank us by not stealing our things while we're sleeping. What is your name?"

"I do not steal!" Standing on her lap as tall as he could, he bowed. "I only borrow, princess. I am called Purloin."

Rudy laughed, because he knew the word purloin meant to steal. "Purloin, it's Rudy. Don't you remember me?"

Purloin's eyes grew large and round as his tiny little fingers fluttered in the air. "Rudy! Yes, I remember! I rescued you and you gave me a great gift." He pulled a small magnifying glass out of his pocket. "I still have it!" He ran to Rudy and jumped into his arms.

Tomtee, who didn't want to hear of Purloin's heroics, snarled, "What happened to you? Why are you covered with more mud than usual?"

"I was attacked by a wild beast! I've never seen such a monster, and I didn't even do a thing to make it mad. It just attacked me."

Tomtee's eyes narrowed. "No furlet has ever been innocent. They lie! Matina made me realize that you couldn't have cut down the forest, but I am still not convinced that you and your primitive friends didn't have something to do with it." Turning to Matina he added, "You may be right that they didn't chop down our forest, but a furlet is always dirty! They steal, and trouble is their middle name."

Josey walked over to Rudy and took Purloin's hand and squeezed it. He was filthy, but he didn't look like a liar or thief. She felt sorry for him.

Purloin cringed when Tomtee spoke. He jumped out of the ground and bowed, "Ah, bosker. I am your servant. I did not see you standing there. Everyone has heard of your generosity."

"It doesn't extend to thieves," Tomtee snapped. "And while we're at it, why didn't the monster eat you?"

Purloin placed his small hands over his eyes and his whole body shook. "Because I told him that someone had poisoned me, and he would die if he ate me. The monster was big, and ugly, and mostly stupid," Purloin squeaked. "Please believe me, Mr. Bosker. We furlets didn't chop your trees. An evil corrupted some of our kind—those afflicted showed the trolls the way in. The trolls are the ones that chopped those trees."

Tomtee couldn't decide whether to believe him or not, but regardless, he had enough of Purloin. They needed to collect firewood as night was quickly coming upon them. Since there was work to be done, the furlet was only too willing to leave. They gathered the wood and made a firepit inside the small cave. Matina used her gift to light the fire and this time there was no explosion, just a nice roaring fire. The tunnel Josey had slid down was a perfect chimney as the smoke spilled upward into it. They sat quietly, resting by the fire's warmth, as all the worrisome shadows were chased away.

Tomtee opened his sack and gave everyone a tiny round cake.

Josey stared at the small cake. "This little cookie is my dinner?"

Rudy squinted his eyebrows together and took a bite. "This is great, it tastes fruity." He brushed the crumbs from his hands. "I can't believe that little cake filled me up."

They heard a noise in the back of the cave and saw a bright light. They all stood ready to defend themselves when a young man emerged from the cave's depths. "You are not going to believe how I got here," exclaimed Billy.

Josey and Rudy rushed to Billy and grabbed him, both trying to talk to him at once.

"Silence!" boomed Tomtee. "Come to the fire and explain everything to us. I take it you are the famous Billy, the other hero of Lusair."

"So glad to meet the other hero." Matina took Billy's hand and led him to the fire. "I am Matina, Princess of the Elmorts, and this is Tomtee, a bosker and friend of the queen. Would you please tell us how you entered our world?"

Billy couldn't sit still. He was proud when he heard he and Rudy were heroes. He stood up and strutted, shaking his dreadlocks. "I guess you could say Rudy and I helped save Lusair." But then he became so excited, the words tumbling so fast out of his mouth, they couldn't understand what he was saying. They had to stop him and have him start over.

"Well, Rudy, you know that my parents work late some days, so instead of going to your house like usual, I decided to work on my science project. I was in my room when out of the blue, a bright circle of light appeared and then I saw the Knight of Light! He said that a new inexperienced questor needed our help and that you and Josey were already here. He also gave me the key that the questor would need." Pulling it out of his shirt and over his head, he showed it to them.

Josey couldn't believe that Billy had also been in Lusair but hung on his every word. She couldn't help herself and interrupted him, "Was the key the size of a football before you entered the circle of light?

"It sure was—I couldn't believe that I had to wear it around my neck. But when I walked into Lusair it became a normal-sized key."

Hands under his chin and eyes turned down, Rudy asked, "Did the knight say anything about my losing the key?"

Billy sat down next to Rudy, slowly drawing out his words, "He sure did."

Dreading what Billy had to say, Rudy waited with his eyes closed so no one would see that he was close to tears.

Silence. More silence. He couldn't take it anymore. He was ready to explode like a volcano when he opened his eyes. Billy's brown hand stretched over to him as he handed him the key. Rudy couldn't believe it. "Why—why are you giving it to me?"

With a laugh, Billy said, "The knight told me that you must be the one to carry the key like you did the first time. He also said that we all make mistakes, but to be more careful this time and protect the key, for it is needed to help the queen."

Matina took Billy's other hand. "Did the knight say anything else about my mother?"

"No, he said that we all need to be with you and help the questor to find her."

Matina sat down by the fire and tried to think about what they were to do. It all seemed so impossible that her mother was missing.

Rudy had trouble talking. He was so grateful they had another key. "Thank you, Billy, but I don't deserve the key. I lost the first one. You need to take care of this one."

Laughing and putting the chain around Rudy's neck he said, "The knight said you would say that, but he has forgiven you and you need to forgive yourself."

Settling down by the fire, Tomtee seemed to accept another mortal in the group and said, "We still have a full day of travel tomorrow. . ."

A low wail rumbled through the cave. Billy, Josey, and Rudy jumped to their feet and grabbed each other's arms when out of the darkness sprang a gigantic cat, its fur spiked like a porcupine and its face like a gorilla's.

Matina put a finger to her mouth, motioning everyone to be quiet. She opened her hand, revealing a red jewel.

The cat sniffed the air and snarled. Josey couldn't believe Matina and Tomtee just sat around the fire while it circled around each one of them. The gigantic cat eyes searched the area for prey but could not see any of them.

First, it walked close to Josey, then Billy and Rudy. It sniffed the ground and their shoes but couldn't sense anything. They all held their breath, too afraid to breathe, and stood rigid as a metal pole sunk in cement. The cat moved back to Tomtee and raised its paw as though to take a swipe, but slowly let it fall to the ground. As it came close to Matina it sat and sniffed and purred. Getting up, it tore at the dirt in frustration, and finally walked away.

Taking a big breath of air, Josey asked, "What was that thing?"

"Why did it just stand there and howl?" Billy asked. "Why didn't it attack us?"

"It is called a tigorila, and it didn't see us because we were invisible. I cloaked us with the magic of this red jewel. This is our shield and protection in case that creature decides to return when we are sleeping. It will see the fire but not us."

Tomtee unrolled his bed roll while the rest arranged theirs in a circle around the fire. “I think it’s time to go to sleep.”

Matina laid the red jewel in the center of the circle and promptly fell asleep.

Josey took her bedroll and placed it in between Billy and Rudy. “Like I’m going to be able to sleep with that thing prowling around.” The fire turned to embers before sleep overtook her.

~ ~ ~

Morning light spread into the cave. Josey opened her eyes but couldn’t move her arms or legs. “Hey, what’s going on?” Panic raced through her; everyone was struggling against the same sticky cord. They were wrapped in a sticky thin rope that wouldn’t budge, mummifying them.

Tomtee’s veins stood out on his neck. “What happened to your protection shield, Matina?”

Her large almond eyes searched frantically for the red stone. “It’s gone!” Matina answered.

Rudy rolled back and forth across the floor. “Billy, maybe you could untie me if I turn around and get close enough. Aggggh!”

From the ceiling of the cave, a giant spider-like creature as big as an air balloon dropped. On each of its eight legs were fingers protruding from the tips. Josey was drawn to the creature’s red beady eyes while fluid dripped from its beaky mouth. It skittered toward Matina.

"Teehee. I have five wonderful morsels for my little ones to eat. It's not often they have royal blood to sup on."

Tomtee struggled against the white cords and shouted, "Redip! What are you doing here? You were banished from the kingdom."

The creature broke into peals of laughter. In a high-pitched voice it said, "The queen's gone! Who's to tell me where I can go?" It arrogantly turned and climbed up through the tunnel. "I will return with my brood. Then you will see where I can go and what I can do!"

Josey closed her eyes. "I'm never going to see home again. Why didn't I learn to listen to my mom? It sure would've been easier than this."

Before anyone could say anything, Matina felt something brush against her arm and twist the cord binding her hands.

"Honorable princess, I will free you," Purloin whispered.

Matina turned and saw the furlet. "Purloin! Hurry! Redip is coming back. She is bringing her brood to make a meal out of us."

Tomtee's eyes narrowed and in a quiet voice asked, "Purloin? Purloin is here? Purloin, did you happen to come by our camp while we slept?"

Purloin worked faster on trying to free Matina. "Oh yes, Mr. Bosker, I wanted to make sure you were all right."

Tomtee's voice started out low but ended in a shout. "And did you happen to see a red jewel when you came to visit?"

Matina's hands were free, and she untied Tomtee while Purloin helped Josey who then helped Billy.

Purloin gulped, "Oh, yes, Mr. Bosker, and a very beautiful stone it was."

Finally free of the cord, Tomtee jumped up and ran over to Purloin. "You stole it, didn't you?"

Purloin stopped and looked at Tomtee. "No, of course not! I don't steal. Never do I steal."

Tomtee picked Purloin up by the scruff of his dirty neck. "I want that red stone."

Dangling in Tomtee's grip, Purloin pulled it out of his pocket. "Oh yes, Mr. Bosker. I came back to return it this morning. Really, I did." He handed Tomtee the red stone.

"Yeah, right!" Tomtee rolled his eyes.

Billy finally was able to untie Rudy and called to Purloin, "Remember me?"

Purloin wiggled out of Tomtee's grasp and ran over to Billy. "I sure do," and he ran up Billy's arm and gave him a furlet's kiss, snuffling at Billy's cheek.

Rubbing the dirt off his cheek, Billy laughed, "Thanks, Purloin."

Rudy jumped up, energized. "Come on, we have to get out of here."

Matina grabbed the red stone and tucked it in her pocket just as the redips surrounded them. So quickly and quietly they moved that no one knew they were there until it was too late. Matina flung her arms out toward them, her hands wide open as fire streamed from her palms. The redips skittered backward to avoid the fire. They squealed with anger but left a path for the group to run out of the cave. Making their escape, they didn't stop until two hills were behind them. There were mountains of rocks as far as they could see. Big, little, middle-sized rocks piled everywhere. Some were so huge they blotted out the sun, casting shadows on smaller piles.

The sun was high in the sky when Josey sat down. "Isn't there anything in Lusair other than rocks?"

Just as Josey finished, squat, bearded men with more wrinkles than prunes surrounded them with huge spears. Matina and Tomtee angrily shoved the spears away. Bristling, the group tightened their circle.

"Hey! Tomtee, don't make them mad." Rudy warned as he gently moved away a spear that was poking his knee.

Tomtee pushed half a dozen of them over, "What do you think you're doing? This is the princess, and I am a bosker! How dare you treat us this way!"

Josey closed her eyes and thought, *Be nice!* Nothing happened. She opened her eyes. The small people stood awkwardly as if not sure what to do next. Matina sat on a rock with her head held high and gestured for one small person to speak.

The tallest of them stood boldly in front of Matina. His face reddened with anger, the spokesperson spat out each word. "The dwarfs no longer bow to your people! Your people no longer govern. They let evil spread! You refuse to rule so we decided to rule Lusair ourselves."

Rudy asked, "Is Dinky with you? I don't see him."

Startled, the leader asked, "Who are you that you know Dinky?"

"I am Rudy. . ."

All the dwarves ran to embrace Rudy. "Dinky has told us so much about you. He is in the Blue Mountains helping Nipron."

Red faced, Rudy gently pushed them away and pointed to Billy. "Billy was with me when. . ." He didn't get a chance to finish as they all ran to Billy for his turn at the greeting.

"Did Dinky tell you how much I admired his magic hammer?" Billy said between hugs.

Matina had bowed her head and was silent for a long time. In a whisper, she said, "Things will change once we go to the questor's mountain and find the queen."

"If you find her," the spokesman snarled.

Tomtee snatched him by the collar. "There are no 'ifs' about it. We will find the queen." He pulled the dwarf up till they were nose to nose. "Have you forgotten the pledge to the land? You are not taking care of it. What kind of rule will you have? One of greed? Sacrificing the land? To help who? Yourselves?"

The dwarf sputtered, "We have rights…"

Tomtee dropped him and threw his hands in the air. "Rights! What rights? Rights to be like the elmorts and do what you want?" Tomtee's dark eyes became darker as he slowly uttered each word, "Or do you want war! You know the boskers will never bow to your rule."

The dwarf rubbed his neck and gathered the others for a brief conference. Finally, the tall one spoke. "We will help you travel to the mountain. All mining will cease for a time, until we see if the queen is found, and the evil is taken from the land."

Tomtee told everyone to link hands.

The tall dwarf raised his spear and plunged it into the rock. The rock cracked and a fluid blue light streaked toward Josey and her group. The blue light surrounded and enveloped them and made them a part of its energy. Immediately, they moved. They moved so fast that Josey felt her body stretch —stretch until she was sure that she was a hundred feet long. Then, just as quickly, they stood in shadows at the base of a mountain.

"Wow! How'd we get here?" Josey gawked. "And don't say I didn't listen, because the only explanation I heard was, 'hang on'."

"Tomtee didn't have time to explain to you what was going to happen." Matina patted Josey's shoulder. "When the dwarf plunged his spear in the rock, he called the blufenul to transport us here."

"Blufenul? What the heck is a blufenul?" Josey asked. "It didn't feel like I was getting into anything or going anywhere. One minute we stood with dwarfs, the next minute I was surrounded by blue light that seemed to stretch me from here Tuesday."

Rudy explained, remembering what Dinky had told them. "The blufenul is magic that lives within the rock formation and is constantly moving. The dwarfs use it to travel just like we did. They call it forth by plunging their spear into the rock. It is one of the gifts that the Knight of Light gave them."

Billy looked up at the mountain. "Are we going to have to climb that?"

"Yes, those blasted dwarves didn't drop us at the nearby questors' tower." Angrily, Tomtee took a long rope out of his backpack. Tie this around yourselves and put on some warmer clothes. You're going to need them on the mountain."

Tomtee tied the rope to himself then checked the others to make sure they also connected.

"How will this rope help?" Josey asked.

"We are going to fly closer to the mountain top," Tomtee said.

“Flying?” Josey’s words were lost as everyone was whisked away.

CHAPTER 5

"Did I miss something again?" Snow swirled in the air, covering Josey's black hair with white. "How'd we get up here?"

"We flew," Rudy explained.

"I sure didn't see any window." No one answered as the wind blew Josey's words away.

Tomtee motioned for everyone to put their hands on the shoulders of the person in front of them. The wind watered their eyes and stung their cheeks as they walked along the wide stony ledge.

The slippery snow made the rocky obstacles all the more dangerous. Rudy lost his footing and began to slide off the ledge. He was desperately windmilling his arms, trying to find balance. In his struggle, Rudy managed to knock Josey and Billy off balance too. Josey lost her feet from underneath her, but Billy grabbed a niche in the wall and hung on for dear life. Rudy and Josey were both dangling in the air above a deep and jagged canyon. Their screams for help went unheard as the roaring wind stole their voices from the air. Billy's muscles were straining as he held onto the crack in the mountain wall, and his feet began to slide. Tomtee did not hear any of the cries but suddenly felt himself being pulled to the edge of the cliff. He turned and saw what had happened. Clicking his fingers, he transported all three adventures to a safe, stable part of the path. In their fearful exhaustion, they immediately collapsed onto the rest of the party.

"Get off of me," Tomtee said in a muffled voice.

Untangling herself, Josey untied her rope and stepped in front of the others. Matina stood up, and then Billy, and then Rudy rolled off Tomtee.

Rudy's sides heaved as he gasped for breath. "I thought we were goners. I lost my grip and slid right off the ledge."

Josey was still trembling. "And you pulled me right with you. I've never been so scared in all my life. How did we get back up here?"

Matina looked around waiting for everyone to feel secure on the ledge. "Remember Grandmother said that Tomtee had magic? Well, he just clicked his fingers and here you are."

They were standing underneath an overhang while Josey took deep breaths, gradually stopping her shaking. She stood, looking around and feeling the grooves of the overhang's wall. Slowly she leant into it, feeling her weight shift into the rocky surface. The nearby storm grew louder and louder as if searching for them.

"What do we do now? The wall behind Josey ends the trail. Are you sure this is the way, Matina?" Tomtee asked.

"The wall is not solid. It's an illusion."

Josey leaned against the wall. "No illusion here."

Matina looked around at Tomtee but insisted it was an illusion. "Grandmother told me I can see through illusions."

"Hey, where'd Josey go?" Rudy asked.

As if to answer, Josey's head poked through the rock wall. "Matina, you're right!"

"Aghh!" they chorused, all except Matina who simply smiled.

Josey grabbed Matina's hand, who grabbed Tomtee's arm, who grabbed Billy, who grabbed Rudy's hand, and pulled them through the wall.

"Wow! No snow! No wind! Look, three suns! And the two moons—it looks like I could reach out and touch the one closest to us." Billy waved his arms. "Did you ever see so many stars out in the daytime?"

"Yeah, and no ledge—we're on solid ground," said Rudy.

Josey was in awe at the swirling colors of pink, purple, green, and white clouds. The hills and valleys were a blue-green, lined with towering green pines and rivers winding through them. In the distance stood a very tall tower that was circular and black. It stood alone, like a sentinel standing guard.

Rudy asked, "What do you suppose that tower is doing out here in the middle of nowhere all alone?"

"It is the questor's home. When he is not helping the land or others, he comes here for rest and study."

They walked toward the tower and wandered into an orchard of fruit trees. The apples, peaches, and plums were as big as basketballs, just waiting to be picked.

"Do you think just one of these could feed all of us? Let's test it with the peach!" Rudy exclaimed as he took out his sword and sliced a huge peach into pieces.

"This is the biggest piece of fruit I've had in my life," sighed Billy between juicy bites.

Deciding to plant the leftover seed, Tomtee took a small shovel from his backpack and started digging. Finally, the hole was big enough for the pit of the peach and he covered it with dirt. No sooner was it covered, than a sprout emerged and a leaf opened.

Sneaking around the trees were huge fruit rattytats who pounced on the group and pinned them to the ground. They were large, fat—snarling and snapping as they bared their big teeth.

Josey held her breath as the yellow eyed rattytats breathed rank air onto her face.

"Who said that you could steal our fruit?" He had a black patch on one of his eyes and a red scarf wrapped around his forehead.

Struggling against his weight she said, "We didn't know it was your fruit. We didn't see any houses or signs that said, 'do not pick,' so we helped ourselves."

"Ha, that's where you messed up. We've laid claim to these trees and no one else is allowed to eat from them."

The rattytat with the black hat laughed hideously. Rudy struggled to break free but failed. After twisting back and forth he was able to pull his sword free and plunge it into the rattytat's leg. Screaming, it let him go and ran away.

Rudy then ran to Matina and threatened more heroics, but the rattytat saw the sword and danced away. The other two also let go of Josey and Billy. All ran away except one—the rattytat that Tomtee was able to overcome and sit on.

"What do you want me to do with this one?" Tomtee asked.

Matina stomped over and began her performance. "I am the Princess of the Elmorts! You better leave us alone. Tomtee—let him up so he can join his creepy friends."

Tomtee got off from him, and the rattytat scurried away, yelling to his friends, “We have to get out of here, it’s the Princess of the Elmorts. She’s going to send an army to destroy us. Run, run for your lives!”

“Ha, it seems he doesn’t listen very well either. Let’s get out of here before they come back,” Matina said.

They hurried on and soon came to fields of butterflies that flew into the air as they approached. The air was filled with beautiful colors that fluttered and glowed in a circle of light as they flew away. “I’ve never had butterflies flutter around my head!” Josey said. “Look! They’ve made a necklace pattern on my tunic.”

An enormous shadow loomed over Josey. In one swoop, it gathered the five of them in its hand and carried them toward the lone tower in the desert a great distance away, holding them gently in wooden hands that swung back and forth like a pendulum.

The landscape blurred in her vision as Josey twisted around and tried to look at the creature, but she only caught glimpses of shaggy brown bark and bulging yellow marble eyes. When she looked down, she didn’t see feet, but tree bark legs walking. “We must be a hundred feet up in the air.” She held her head up and tried to focus her eyes on the black tower that came into view and spiraled up into the clouds, but the swinging back and forth made her dizzy.

The creature arrived at the lone black tower and reached his arm midway up the tower. A door appeared and a walkway sprung out. It was like a highway hanging in space. They were carefully placed on the surface.

“Go!” the giant thundered.

Without a glance at the creature, Josey ran lickety-split into the open door of the tower, and everyone quickly followed. She leaned against the wall and slid to the floor. “Twice I thought I was going to die out there.”

“Me too! But wow, look at this! Everything is glass.” Billy pounded on the wall and then ran to the banister. “Look, even the banister is glass! This spiral staircase is so long it must go to the basement.”

Josey shook her head as Billy’s voice echoed and chimed in her ears.

Tomtee put his hand over Billy’s mouth and whispered, “Talk quietly. The glass magnifies our voices.”

Her dizziness passed and Josey looked around. Golden rays of sun streamed through the walls and ceiling. “How come the outside is black, but in here we can see right through the walls?”

Matina walked to a doorway and into a room. Next to the window a four-foot picture of her grandmother was on the wall.

Josey followed. “Your grandmother was very beautiful. I assume that is your grandmother because the woman in the picture is wearing the same ring that you have on.”

Matina looked down at the ring and then touched the one in the picture. She thought she saw the ring in the picture glow then fade away.

Tomtee leaned over the banister rail and pointed at a circle of steps going down, down, down. "Let's find the questor."

Josey was looking out the window at the mountain. She turned around to say something to Matina, but she was gone. Hurrying to the doorway, she watched the others descend the stairway before she started her walk down. *They could have told me they were leaving. Wonder what we'll find at the bottom.* She investigated the different rooms that splintered off the steps. Each had curved walls and curved windows that shined squeaky clean. *No one can live in a place this clean,* she thought.

Josey came to the last step that led into a large circular room. Books lay everywhere, in the middle of the floor, on the shelves, on the tables. Stacks and stacks of books reached the ceiling. The group wandered through the maze of books when they came face to face with a small purple creature.

"Aghh!" they chorused.

Josey caught up in time to see Billy spin around and run straight into Rudy, who fell onto a pile of books. Tomtee grabbed Matina to protect her when they tripped against a bookcase that rocked back and forth, raining books from its top. The purple creature turned left then right, left then right, unsure which way to go. Its large round eyes bulged under the crease of its brow.

A white light appeared. All motion stopped. Books hung in midair. Rudy was on his knees with his hands over his head. Matina balanced on one foot, her arms flung out, holding on to Tomtee. Billy was frozen into a jump over a fallen table and Josey was frozen in the doorway.

In the next instant, Josey and her friends found themselves in front of a towering questor. His eyes glowed like dark pools under white bushy eyebrows. Josey saw a hint of a smile in the wooly beard and felt at ease.

"So, you dare enter my tower."

The small purple thing poked its head out from behind the questor.

"Aghh!" they chorused again.

The questor clapped his large hands. "Stop that! There is nothing to be afraid of! Cully, come out and introduce yourself!"

The skinny purple creature with large bulging eyes stepped out from behind the questor. "I am Cully. A reformed goblin." He clasped his large hands together and smiled, exposing large yellow teeth.

"Why are you purple?" Billy asked.

Cully squinted one eye and looked at the questor, hesitant to say anything.

The questor said, "That was an accident. When I was first on my own and performing the necessary spells to help Cully, a flower…a flower fell into the potion…"

Cully turned and faced the group and in a raspy whisper said, "He was trying to improve on the formula instead of following it."

"Now, now Cully, I said that I would redo the formula, no need to go into that."

Matina timidly took the ring off her finger and placed it on the table.

The questor's eyes widened. "How is the queen?"

"My mother is now the queen and has been stolen away!" Matina picked up the ring and twisted it back and forth between her fingers. She went on telling him about the disappearance of her mother. "Grandmother gave me the ring to show you so that you would help—she said you would know where to find her."

The questor's face turned from a rosy pink to a pasty white. "Take care of our guests, Cully." With a loud pop the questor disappeared.

"What's the matter with him?" Josey asked.

"He needs a few minutes alone. It's quite a shock seeing you, Matina, for you look just like your grandmother. My master and your mother grew up together and were very close when they were young. They knew from the start their destinies ran in different directions and finally parted," said Cully.

"What does the ring mean?" Tomtee asked.

"Ah, they made a pact when they were young that if either of them needed help, they would help, no matter what.

The questor appeared, wringing his hands, weeping. "I'm so sorry, Matina, but I have lost my key that will enable me to protect you."

Cully hurried to his defense. "It wasn't his fault. A huge flood of water washed off the mountain and filled the tower, submerging it for hours. We barely survived. Then a strong wind rushed through and drove us and everything in the tower out. We tumbled head over heels for a long time. It was so odd."

Throwing his hands in the air the questor continued, "It took us weeks to find the things that we needed to gather back into the tower."

Josey was listening intently and asked, "Why didn't you just use your magic to bring everything in the tower?"

In a whispered voice, his head in his hands, the questor said, "For some reason when I lost the key, I lost my power."

Finally, it dawned on Rudy that the questor needed the key. "I have the key! The Knight of Light sent it to you. I had a key but lost it to a mewling and the knight sent Billy with this key." In his desperation to help the questor, he struggled to take it off.

The questor's trembling hand took the key and placed it around his neck. "I shall return," he whispered as he disappeared in a flash.

"*Now* where did he go?" asked Billy.

“I’m not sure, but I would guess he is searching for the queen,” Cully replied.

In another flash of light, the questor reappeared. His torn robe smelled of smoke. His beard had been singed and was still smoking while he staggered to the table. “I know where your mother is being held. It is an evil place.” He cradled his soot-covered face in his hands and in an anguished voice said, “I tried to rescue her. I, a master questor, can do nothing! Nothing.”

CHAPTER 6

Tears spilled from Matina's eyes. She placed her hand in the questor's. "There must be something we can do."

From his table, the questor turned his grief-stricken face toward her. "You sound like your grandmother." Slowly he added, "Snivel the Delf has your mother."

"Who is Snivel?" Tomtee asked.

The questor's voice cracked and boomed, "An old delf, but not as old as the elmorts. Snivel is the last of its kind. A group of elves were angry because the elmorts grew in numbers. Their magic became vital to Lusair, more so than the elves. In a jealous rage, the elves attempted to create something better than an elmort. It was a disaster. Their creation turned on them and almost destroyed them. That's why elves are not seen today. They are hiding from the old delf. It's hideous, with huge bony features lining its back, and its skinny legs are bowed under its weight. And it has huge wings like sails on a ship. Its jaw opens wide to breathe fire."

The questor's fingers brushed the red embers from his beard. "The old delf who took your mother is evil and powerful. Its evil is so great that you feel its presence whenever it passes by. I watched him for a long time, and he constantly sings this song."

I, Snivel the Delf, await rebirth,
the queen is a jewel no one can unearth.
For now, I cannot sleep or eat,
slowly, I become more weak.
The pure of heart can overcome,
and make is so the delf's undone.
That is, if one can find the jewel,
before the delf makes it his tool.

Rudy shook his head. The song had almost lulled him to sleep. "What does it mean?"

"I am certain your mother is the key. She is the tool he needs for renewing his strength and magic. It could mean that Snivel is dying." Rubbing the tears away, he continued, "When he renews his youth, he renews his power. With that power he will gain control over Lusair. But he must wait until that time when the two moons pass over each other—then he will utter his spell.

I know that Snivel turned your mother into a jewel and hid her very carefully among his hoard. The key showed me, but the image would not last." The questor threw up his hands. "Where it is I do not know. What kind of jewel it is, I do not know."

"Why were you not able to conquer his evil?" Tomtee asked.

Questor bowed his head. "Only those pure of heart can defeat him." Promptly he had an idea. "You will all go to Snivel's cavern. You five are going on a hunt. A hunt to find the queen."

Everyone looked at everyone else. "Now wait a minute, none of us are perfect. I certainly am not pure of heart so it can't be me." Josey felt her face and her ears heat to a red glow. "Tell them, Rudy. I don't listen very well, and I say I can do things I can't."

"She's telling the truth—besides, are you crazy? You come back with your beard smoking and your robe all torn to pieces. What do you think we can do?"

Matina put her hand around Josey's shoulder. "Josey, none of us are perfect, but don't you remember what Grandmother said? I won't be able to find my mother without you."

Josey stammered, "But, but—what am I supposed to do?"

The questor's fingers combed through his beard. He turned from the group, muttering to himself, "They need training with the swords of light. They'll also need the glow rock headbands to see inside the cavern…six should do…"

Cully interrupted with a squeak. "I heard you say six. Why do you need six?"

"Because you are going with them."

Cully turned a sickly pink and ran up to the questor, "But master. . . "

"No buts! They will need your help."

"Master. . ."

The questor ignored Cully's plea. "Snivel creates illusions. You, Matina, can see through most, but not all of them. Tomtee, your magic will be necessary, for this is a dangerous journey"

"Master. . ."

The questor ignored Cully and continued, "You must have your wits about you, for it is dangerous and I won't be able to help you very much."

"Master. . ."

The questor lost all patience and shouted, "What is it, Cully?"

"Please, Master, if you would remove your foot from mine."

"Oh, sorry about that." He bent down and patted Cully on the head. "Do you have any other questions?"

Cully shook his head no and limped around the table to join the others.

"Now before you leave you will need to be trained to defend yourselves. Take these."

Six small swords in their scabbards hovered before them. The black hilts were carved with hundreds of tiny glittering stars. The questor drew one of the swords. All that came out was one hilt with no blade. He made a slashing motion. A sharp brilliant white light emitted from its hilt. "Watch that table in the corner," he instructed.

He pointed the sword at the table and swished it in the air in a chopping motion. The table collapsed in two. "Now, I will show you what happens when the blade comes in contact with an object." He touched the tip of the glowing blade to the table. It disappeared before their eyes.

"What happened? Did it just disappear and reappear somewhere else?" asked Rudy.

"No, it was completely destroyed." The questor tapped the bottom of the hilt and the light disappeared.

"You have three days to become skilled in the use of these swords. You will practice from sunup till sundown."

Josey placed her hands on her hips. "Are you nuts? We could kill or destroy each other!"

The questor unsheathed the sword hilt and its brilliant white light flowed directly at Josey. "Do you think I would put you in danger? During practice, these swords of light will function like regular swords, helping you to become efficient in their use for your quest ahead."

Everyone screamed and ducked. Everyone but Josey, she couldn't move. She closed her eyes and felt the sharp light flow around her. It was like the wind softly touching her skin. Nothing happened.

Josey opened her eyes looked at herself. "I'm still here, you didn't va—va—vaporize me!"

"Don't be foolish. I've placed a spell on the swords to protect ALL OF YOU. I don't want you to accidentally trip and become dust."

Rudy and Billy each grabbed one. Rudy handed the sword he had taken from the palace to the questor. "I'd prefer yours—this one is rather outdated. When do we start?"

They were ushered outside, and the questor pointed to a flat brown area. "You will begin when we get there."

"That must be five miles away!" Josey said.

"You don't seriously think I would let you bang those swords anywhere near my tower, do you?"

The questor blinked his eyes and they arrived at the dirt arena with swords in hand. "Do not eat or sleep without your swords. Cully, you team up with Josey, and Matina you partner with Rudy. Tomtee, you team up with Billy and then take turns with the others. Being a bosker, Tomtee needs no training, so he will take turns fighting all of you in order to give you practice with a master."

Matina and Rudy went to work. Matina quickly displayed her mastery. Rudy, on the other hand, waved the sword in the air as though it were a conductor's baton, whipping it back and forth. Matina had practiced sword fighting from the time she was five years old. She would lunge and hit Rudy in the chest, sending him head over heels backwards. Once he learned to avoid her thrusts, he tried lunges of his own, but would trip and fall.

Billy was dancing around Tomtee, avoiding all his lunges.

Josey asked Cully if he was ready. In answer he let out a yell and charged. She stepped aside and tripped him.

"That's not fair," Cully yelled.

"Anything is fair," the questor snapped. "Now get up and fight."

Josey stood ready as Cully got up and held his blade high. She brought her blade into his stomach, and it flipped him onto his back. She ran over to see if he was okay. Before she knew it, Cully whipped his blade behind her knees, bringing her to the ground. She rolled away and jumped up only to face his blade at her neck. She fell backward and kicked the blade out of his hand.

"Josey! Whoever taught you to fight?" Tomtee asked.

"I've been taking Tae Kwon Do at school."

Rudy interrupted. "Yeah, she's the best in the class, except for me. I started taking it after Dinky showed me some of the moves."

"What is this twit-can-do stuff?" Cully snapped.

Josey laughed. “Tae Kwon Do! It’s a special defense exercise.”

“If you are quite through, I expect you to resume your work,” said the questor.

They practiced all day and well into the night. The next day they were transported from their beds to the dirt arena with swords in hand.

“Hey, don’t we even get breakfast?” asked Josey.

The questor appeared and said, “You need to work up an appetite first.”

Once again, they practiced all day with only a few quick breaks for meals. The questor drove them to exhaustion. Slowly the sun met the earth and torches lit their fighting arena. They looked at the moons as they seemed to be getting closer.

Matina asked, “Will we be trained in time so that we can rescue Mother?”

The quester patted her shoulder and assured her there was plenty of time. After a hearty meal, the questor told them he had to leave for a short time, but they were to practice. When he left, they all went into the center of the ring and collapsed.

“I can’t move a muscle,” Rudy said.

“My everything hurts,” Cully added.

“Look!” Matina cried.

In the darkness loomed four massive, hairy, creatures. Long fangs glittered in the light of the torches and their star-shaped claws clattered like a stick on a wheel spoke. They slowly crept forward with menacing growls and angry eyes.

"We better use our swords, or we're finished," Tomtee cried.

Six swords blazed together and were aimed at the hairy creatures. Instantly the creatures were vaporized in a puff of smoke.

"That was close. Oh no!" Matina yelled.

Six gigantic bats with knives on their wings swooped down toward them. The party all fell to the ground as the bats flew over them. The bats turned to come at them again.

Tomtee yelled, "Roll on your back and raise your swords." Again, the blades went to work. Before they could even stand up, monstrous worms burst through the dirt with gaping mouths. Quickly they used their blades and once again the monsters disappeared.

Then nothing. Nothing but eerie quiet. Drenched with sweat, they fell against a brick wall.

"Did. . .did. . ." Cully stammered.

"Yes, we did. We destroyed them all," Tomtee said.

"Hey, where'd this wall come from?" Josey asked.

Before anyone could answer, the wall grew like a snake surrounding them. It moved inward and shrank the area where they stood, continuing its approach.

“What should we do? Pretty soon we’ll be crushed!” Matina yelled.

“The swords! Let’s hold them all in one spot. Maybe we can blast a hole through it,” Tomtee cried.

Bricks flew in the air as they scrambled out of the hole and ran smack into the questor.

“Wait a minute,” Josey snapped. “Did you create all those monsters we blew away?”

“Yes, indeed. Seems that you lot decided you needed a rest. You will not have that chance where you’re going.”

The surprise attacks did not let up. During the night when they were just falling asleep, they heard a great roar. Grabbing their swords, they all ran out into the hall to face ten-foot-tall bear with long pointy teeth that glinted in the dim light. His paws and claws were bigger than baseball mitts. Pulling their hilts out and swishing the brilliant light, they immediately destroyed the bear.

~ ~ ~

The next bleary-eyed morning they arrived at the breakfast table, which promptly turned into a giant lizard. Josey and the others tipped chairs over trying to scramble out of the way. They unsheathed their swords and again vaporized it on the spot.

Cully, grouchy from having his sleep disturbed, said, “Can’t even eat breakfast in peace.”

Josey and Rudy and Billy waited before they picked up their chairs, anticipating another threat. They finally sat down and began eating once again. Josey ate slowly, alert and waiting. She couldn't believe how Rudy and Billy ate, shoveling food in their mouth as though it were their last meal. As soon as everyone finished eating, and before they had a chance to leave the table, they were whisked to the arena and their practice began once more.

Rudy decided to take a break and walked to a cluster of pine trees and sat down. "It's too hot."

Tomtee walked over to him and quietly told him to get back to work. "It will be hotter where we are going."

Rudy stood up and made the sign of Zorro over his head. "To free…" he began, just as a huge branch fell on top of Rudy and Tomtee.

CHAPTER 7

Josey and the others saw what happened and ran to help. “Are you guys okay?”

They pulled the large pine branches away from Tomtee and Rudy. Spitting out pine needles and brushing them out of his hair, Rudy waved his sword around again. Everyone including Tomtee ran away from him. *Whoosh*—more pine branches covered Rudy.

Tomtee yelled, “Do not—I repeat—do not wave that sword about!!”

Once uncovered, Rudy sheathed his sword. He brushed pine needles from his hair and out of his ears. "Sorry, guess we have to be careful where we point these things."

All day they combated creatures that appeared out of nowhere. At the end of the day, the questor had prepared a banquet fit for a king. Everyone was too tired to enjoy the delicious food—everyone but Rudy and Billy.

The next morning was their last day of practice. Breakfast was sparse. They arrived at the arena and were immediately set upon by wolves walking upright. Somehow Billy became separated from the others. The wolves ran toward him as he whipped his sword in the air and waved the brilliant light. Nothing happened except fur flew from the wolves' hides. They still ran toward him. Again, he pointed the brilliant sharp light toward them. It washed over them. More fur flew in the air, but they kept coming. The others saw what was happening and ran to help, swords poised to fight. Finally, the enemy disappeared, but only when the five swords fused together to destroy the wolves.

Billy shook his sword. "My sword must not work. I couldn't destroy those wolves."

Tomtee took Billy's weapon and waved it toward a rock. Chips splintered off in a brilliant explosion. Tomtee tried his own sword and the same thing happened, only a few rocks splintered off. He then used Billy's sword and his together and waved them toward a rock. The rock split open. He took everyone's swords and waved them toward the broken rock. The rock disappeared. Everyone stood quietly trying to figure out what was wrong.

Josey figured out what was happening. "I got it! Remember when Rudy waved his sword in the air under the pine tree? Well, one sword will only cause a little damage, but you need them all to work together to vaporize monsters."

"How come we didn't need them all together before?" Cully demanded.

Josey thought about the past few days. "But we did use them all together, every single time. Think about it. This is the first time that one of us was separated from the others."

"You're right," said Matina. She described each monster they had encountered and how their swords working together destroyed them.

Suddenly a swarm of killer bees surrounded them. They put their swords together and the bees vanished. No sooner were the bees gone, then a gigantic beetle appeared, then a werewolf, and a vampire. On and on monsters appeared and were destroyed by the brilliant light of the swords.

"This is boring," Josey said.

Instantly, the questor appeared by her side. "I'm glad you're bored! At least you don't run screaming into the night when you see a horrible creature. You should have learned that you need to use your swords together in order to destroy something. That is because you need to work as a team and not alone. Even if there are only two or three of you using the sword, when you work together you can accomplish anything. Remember that."

They all laughed. It was true they had become warriors. The next morning it was time for them to leave. The questor paced, his hands clasped behind him, and watched them pack.

"We're ready," Josey said.

The questor brushed his fingers through his beard, then stopped and folded his arms. "Remember, this is not a game. You must keep your wits about you and work together. Your practice may have made things appear to be too easy. It won't be easy."

The questor paused and his voice came out low and husky. "I know you're ready. Tomtee, you will lead this group. If you think it is too risky—well, you know what to do." Then with a wave of his hand they were transported close to Snivel's lair.

The whole world looked like wilted lettuce. Hazy, gray clouds hid the sun. Steam oozed from the earth in spurts, creating a constant mist.

Rudy held his nose. "Yuck! Smells like a rotten potato!"

"Look at those twisted trees," Josey said. "It's like they're crying out in pain."

Matina gazed at the sky where the two moons appeared. A sickly white and a dead tree rose hundreds of feet in the air. "Look how close those two moons are, they're almost touching."

They were putting their moonstone headbands on and the gloomy mist was brightening when they saw six of the twisted trees starting to move.

“Snakes,” Josey cried.

“Quick, use your swords!” Tomtee cried.

The snakes were quick as lightning. One grabbed Josey’s leg before she could even unsheathe her sword. It wound its body around her quicker than a drop of water falling to the ground and flicked her sword away with its tongue.

Cully’s sword was yanked out of his hand by the snake’s tail. In a blink of an eye, it wrapped itself around him.

Tomtee grabbed the fallen swords and he and Billy ran close to Cully and Josey as their swords blazed white. Rudy and Matina were back-to-back, destroying the other snakes, before they could reach them.

Josey gasped for air. “Whew! Thanks! I thought I was a goner!”

They saw the entrance to the cave and were about to run into it when fire and smoke came rolling out. The small group spread apart as they quickly ran away in opposite directions. Tomtee and Cully and Billy went left while Matina Josey and Rudy ran right. A heavy mist arose, creating a thick fog.

Tomtee grabbed Cully and Billy and told them to put on the cuff bracelets that would link them together.

“We are not children…” The rest came out muffled as Tomtee covered Cully’s mouth.

Tomtee drew Cully and Billy so close to him that they bumped heads. In a whisper he said, “Don’t say a word. Snivel knows we are here and is listening.”

Not too far away and behind a huge boulder were the other three. Matina whispered, “We can’t stay here—Snivel will find us. Let’s crawl out but hang on to each other’s hands so we know where each of us are.”

Rudy pulled Matina back and asked, “How are we going to find the others?”

“We’ll figure it out, but if we have to talk to each other, remember to whisper in our ears.”

They crawled out from behind the boulder and stood looking around. Everything was like a blank sheet of white paper. They could not see each other. Rudy pulled Matina’s hand up to his eye and then pulled her closer so he could whisper in her ear. “Should we take off our headbands?”

Matina whispered, “Yes.” They all took off their headbands.

The white mist became muddy with light and dark shades of shapes, but they could not make out what they were looking at. At least they could see each other’s shape and didn’t need to hold hands.

Josey felt something beginning to crawl on her tennis shoe. She pulled out her sword and swished until the brilliant light appeared and pointed it toward the ground. Scorpions were everywhere. In a panicked whisper she said, “Guys, use your swords—quickly!”

Rudy and Matina followed Josey's lead. Both gasped when they saw hundreds of scorpions around their feet. They put their swords together and twirled about like a merry-go-round until all those creepy crawlies disappeared.

Meanwhile Tomtee, Cully, and Billy were using their swords to combat huge ants that were trying to eat their clothes. Finally, Billy grabbed all three swords and waved them all over the three's bodies. He then twirled in a circle until all the ants disappeared.

Tomtee took his sword back whispering, "Thank you, Billy."

Slowly the mist began to lift, and they were able to see where they were. They were not by the entrance of the cave, but in a jungle of wild plants and humongous vines that fell from the gigantic trees. They began trying to find the others and started calling their names.

"We're here!" yelled Matina.

Rudy and Josey came running, following Matina through the vines and a giant leaf plant.

With his hands on his knees and gasping for breath, Rudy asked, "How did you find us? We just started running once we could see and heard you calling."

Cully was nervous being in between all the leaves and vines and kept a leery eye out for enemies. "We just appeared here after the mist lifted. Where do you think we are?"

"Like we know," Tomtee drolled. "I think Snivel transported us away from the entrance of the cave."

Josey pulled at Billy's shirt. "What happened to your clothes? They're torn to bits!"

Cully put his hand through a hole in his shirt. "Billy saved us from huge ants that wanted to eat all our clothes!"

"This is a strange part of Lusair, and I am sure Snivel sent them," Tomtee mused.

"We had scorpions trying to get us. There must have been billions! It's a good thing we have these swords." Josey's words slowed and grew softer, "I wonder if I'll ever see home again."

"Why didn't Snivel just burn us up instead of sending all those things after us?" asked Cully.

Tomtee narrowed his eyes and frowned at Cully. "Like we know… or do we?"

"What's that supposed to mean?" asked Cully.

Tomtee slowly walked in a circle, pointing his finger this way and that. "Suppose he is afraid of the magic we have. Suppose his magic is dying like the questor said, and suppose he used up a lot of his magic and is weak right now."

"I sure would hate to meet him when he was strong. He caused that mist and those things to attack us, so he can't be that weak," said Billy.

Tomtee kept walking. "What if after each attack he needs time to regenerate, and that's why he moved us further away?"

“You could be right, but how do we get back to the entrance of the cave?” Matina asked.

“What if we try and remember what it looked like when the questor placed us in front of the entrance?” Tomtee suggested.

Josey shuddered. “I remembered the trees that turned into snakes, and it stank, stank, stank.”

“Yeah, and the air was hazy with a red tinge to it,” added Billy.

“I saw the two moons over my shoulder,” said Matina.

Tomtee interrupted, “Which shoulder, Matina?”

She thought awhile and then said, “My right shoulder.”

He placed Matina in front of himself. “Think hard, what else did you see?”

“I saw bones everywhere and a dead tree. The tree was so tall that it looked like it could almost touch the two moons.”

Tomtee could hardly contain his excitement. “Someone needs to climb to the top of this tree and see if they can see that dead tree!”

No one spoke and no one moved. They all looked up at the tall tree and then at Tomtee like he was crazy.

Finally, Rudy spoke. “I used to be afraid to climb higher than two pairs of socks, but I guess I could give it a try.”

CHAPTER 8

No one seemed to object or try and stop him, so Rudy shrugged his shoulders and began the climb. It was fairly easy, as there were so many limbs and huge leaves, but the closer he got to the top the harder it became. He looked down at the others—they looked like small toys. His foot slipped and he tumbled back into a giant leaf. Rudy lay there frozen, afraid to move. He finally sat up and stretched his hand to reach the limb. Shakily, he pulled himself up onto the limb and sat awhile. Finally, he began again and reached the top when the wind blew. It tossed the tree limbs back and forth like a pendulum, but he saw the dead tree in the distance. With one hand he pointed. “Can you see which way I am pointing?” he yelled.

“I sure can,” said Tomtee who appeared beside him.

Rudy almost fell, but Tomtee grabbed him. “Why did you have me climb up here if all you had to do was use magic?” Rudy sputtered.

“Because there are times when you need to be reminded that you have to overcome your fear.”

Rudy stared at Tomtee and then burst out laughing, shaking them from their perch. They sailed down the tree safely with Tomtee’s magic.

Once on the ground, Billy ran over to Rudy who slapped his back encouragingly. “You were so brave to climb that high!”

Matina asked Tomtee if he knew how to get back to the entrance. He said he did but that when they got there, they couldn’t talk. They would have to use sign language as Snivel would be able to hear them. “We need to hurry, so link hands and I will transport us, but be very quiet and follow my lead. Put your moonrock headbands on now.”

As soon as they linked hands, Tomtee nodded his head and they arrived at the entrance to the cave. They quickly ran inside, the moon rocks in their headbands flaring even brighter with light. Keeping their swords unsheathed, they walked along the petrified stone path in the long wide tunnel.

Dust swirls clung to their feet as they stepped over the bones littering the passageway.

Josey forgot about not talking. "Snivel could use a cleaning lady."

In a flash, mops and buckets appeared in their empty hands.

"Tomtee! What are you doing? I wish you would give us warning!" Matina hissed.

Cully shook his mop and whispered, "Do you think this is a good idea?"

"It's going to be difficult to use my sword. My hands are full with this mop and bucket," said Billy.

In a snap they were gone.

"Whew, glad you got rid of those things." Rudy grabbed the sword with both hands and looked at Tomtee. "Why are your eyes closed?"

Tomtee opened his eyes. They were red. "Snivel is talking to me." Tomtee's voice was thin and reedy as he struggled to speak. "He sees everyone through my eyes, but he can't read my…"

"What's he got—radar?" Josey asked.

"WHAT ARE YOU DOING HERE?" Tomtee's voice roared, deep and raspy.

"Tomtee, what's wrong?" Matina asked.

Tomtee pulled his sword out of its sheath and swished it until the light came on, then pointed it at Matina. "I WILL ASK YOU ONE MORE TIME. WHAT ARE YOU DOING HERE?"

Cully yelled, "Follow me." They ran away from Tomtee and raced down the tunnel, leaving Tomtee standing still in a trance. Soon, they came to a fork in the tunnel.

"Which way do we go?" asked Cully.

"Like we really know," Josey huffed.

"Let's try the right," Matina said.

They sped off and after a time stopped to catch their breath, when unexpectedly, a large crab-like spider dropped from above.

"Aghh! Redips!" came a unified scream. Their swords were quickly snatched away as the monster spat out a white stream of webbing. With another hiss, it tied Josey up in a sticky web. Before it could spit out more, Billy threw a huge rock that landed in the redip's mouth, while Matina drew her knife and sliced the arm that held the swords. Rudy drew his bow and sent an arrow through its eye, killing the Redip.

Matina took her knife and cut Josey free from the white webbing. They knew they didn't have long before something else happened, so they started running again.

Gasping, Matina looked about. "Cully, what happened to Tomtee? Does Snivel have him?"

Cully shrugged his shoulders. “I’m not sure, but it appears he’s gone. We have to figure out what to do next.”

Tomtee’s voice filled the silence. “Matina, Cully, Josey, Rudy, Billy, where are you?”

They all stopped talking. “Maybe we should wait for him. He sounds normal again.” Rudy said.

Out of nowhere, five golden necklaces appeared at their feet with a note attached. “Put these on! Immediately!” it read.

Josey grabbed a necklace and looked it over. “What the heck?”

“Never mind, Josey. Just do it,” Cully said. “This is from the questor. He must be watching us.”

“I think we should put one of these on Tomtee; I just remembered his sword can’t hurt us. The questor made sure of it, remember?” Josey said. “Tomtee, Tomtee, we’re here!”

Tomtee came running toward them, “I don’t know what came over me! I wouldn’t hurt any of you…” His eyes began to turn red again.

Billy quickly slipped the questor’s necklace over Tomtee’s head. The eerie red faded from his eyes.

“Whew, for a minute, I thought Snivel had me again,” Tomtee gasped.

“The necklace saved you,” Matina said.

"The questor sent them," Cully added. "These necklaces keep Snivel from taking over."

"NOT FOR LONG!"

Matina gasped, "Did you hear that?"

Everyone nodded. A hot sizzling noise alerted them. They spun around and watched a fireball hurling toward them.

Josey had never seen anything move so fast and wondered if she'd just melt. As it sped closer, the light and heat were so intense, she had to close her eyes. Just when she thought it was all over, Josey suddenly felt her body go numb and rigid. She opened her eyes and looked at herself. She was a rock!

Looking up, she watched the ball of flame roll over her. Its roar sounded like a million bees swirling over her head. In the center, the blue and yellow flames danced so brightly they made her eyes water and the tears sizzled on her rock body.

As quickly as it came, the fireball was gone.

Josey asked Tomtee, "How long are we going to be rocks?"

"Until we cool off!"

"Maybe we could make plans," Matina said.

"How are we going to do that with Snivel hearing our every move?" Rudy asked.

"I've got an idea," Matina said. She sang a familiar melody, but no one knew what the words were or what they meant.

She stopped and all was silent. No one spoke, not even Snivel. The rocks cooled and Tomtee turned them back into their human forms.

"Matina," Cully started.

Matina held up her hand for silence.

A low rumbling voice washed over them. "SOOO, YOU THINK YOU CAN FOOL ME! YOU SANG MY MELODY! WHO GAVE IT TO YOU?" The wavering voice came again, but more softly, "I will find you! Then you will tell me the words! Where are you from? What language do you speak?"

Matina leaned toward Tomtee and whispered in his ear. He jerked away and shook his head. Matina placed her hands on her hips and nodded angrily.

Tomtee stood quietly, rubbing his forehead while trying to decide what to do. Finally, Tomtee transformed himself and the others into elmorts.

"What's going on?" Rudy asked. "Hey, my words are coming strangely—but I still understand what I'm saying!"

Matina chuckled, "Snivel cannot understand our ancient language. It is the way we spoke before its kind was created." Matina smoothed her hair and stood straight. "I sang the Dark Elf's song, the one the questor sang, but in the ancient elmort language."

"I knew I had heard those words before," Cully said.

"Tomtee, why didn't you want Matina to change us into elmorts?" Josey asked, shaking the sensation back into her hands from being a rock.

Tomtee hung his head. "It's against the law. Matina said this was an emergency. The council would have to agree with our decision, but I am not so sure."

Matina frowned and pinched her lips together. "This is the only way." Her chin wavered. "There is no other way to get close enough to find and save my mother. Grandmother always said there would be times when rulers must take risks. I'm not a ruler yet, but I need to practice what we believe and not ignore hard decisions."

Tomtee whipped out his helmet made of wood. It had a large red jewel on the top, like the one Matina used in the cave. He disappeared. Everyone looked around and called his name. He suddenly appeared with the helmet in his hand. "I wanted to show you what this helmet would do. It makes you invisible."

He waved his hand and they all had wooden helmets in their hands. "Put them on."

"Hey, Tomtee, I can still see everyone," Billy said.

"Yes, we'll be able to see each other, but no one else will see us, especially Snivel."

"Wow, these are so light. I thought they would be heavy since they're made out of wood," said Josey.

"They are made from a wood called balsa wood. You have to remember, even though Snivel can't see us, he can still hear us when we get close, so you will also have to be very quiet."

"Are these red stones the same as the one you had in the cave?" asked Rudy.

"Yes, now let's get moving. Remember we have to find Mother before the two moons cross over each other," said Matina.

They walked to the end of the tunnel and peered around the cavern. Light bounced from one gold pile to another. Mounds of jewels winked and sparkled from the floor to the ceiling in different sections in the cave.

The humongous delf stood at the far end of the cavern. He looked like a shadow with skin so very thin that it looked like gray tissue. The huge wings sprouting from his back were gaunt with splotches of black which slowly fluttered back and forth. The knot on his forehead glowed a sickly green, then faded when he turned his head. His only tooth, blackened and decayed, curved forward and rested on his chin.

Out of the otherwise toothless mouth came a laugh, "COME OUT AND SHOW YOURSELVES."

Josey felt compelled to obey, and she would have, if she hadn't become a rock again. Tomtee knew he had to do something so that they wouldn't feel the need to obey the delf. No one spoke. Snivel's head swiveled right and left, scanning the cavern for them. He paused upon the rocks and then walked slowly toward them, the mountains of jewels glittering from the torches that lined the cavern.

Josey felt dizzy with fear. *Can he sense that we are rocks?*

Snivel heard a noise, looked up, then grabbed a bat in its flight. After stuffing it in his mouth, blood dribbled around the decayed tooth. He then flew over a mountain of gold to settle on the other side.

The rocks shimmered and soon four elmorts were standing there.

Josey felt sick and hugged her stomach as she bent over. In a whisper she said, "That was disgusting, all that blood gushing from his mouth. Do you think he saw us? I thought we were goners!"

Matina whispered. "We need to put on our helmets before he spots us."

No sooner had the words left Matina's mouth, a shadow came overhead, snatched them up, and flew back over the mountain of jewels.

CHAPTER 9

Snivel dropped them forcefully into a huge cage on top of an endless mound of treasure. Their helmets of invisibility were just outside their cage, just out of their reach.

"This is the biggest bird cage I have ever seen! Look at all the designs in the wiring. They're birds!" said Billy.

Josey stretched her arm through one of the rungs, trying to reach their helmets. It was as if Snivel was taunting them by keeping their helmets so close and yet out of their reach.

"At least we have lots of room, even if there is no floor," Rudy said. "Did you ever think you would be walking on gold and jewels?"

They tried tunneling under the bottom rungs, but all they managed to do was dig a few holes. They stood looking at the endless mounds of gleaming gems—rubies, sapphires, crystals, diamonds, opals, emeralds. Large crowns and flowers made of gold. Gold coins were scattered everywhere. Cully and Billy and Rudy began filling the holes they had dug so that they would be able to walk around their cage without falling. It was useless trying to dig their way out.

"What are we going to do now?" Cully moaned.

Tomtee sat on an enormous diamond, "I think we will have to wait and see what Snivel is going to do next."

Cully looked around at the mounds of treasures. "Where do you think he went?"

Everyone glared at Cully.

"Like we know!" Josey snapped.

Matina stood upon a gold brick that was as large as a suitcase. "At least we have plenty of room to move around in our prison. Tomtee, can't you use your magic to get us out?"

Tomtee shook his head, "This is Snivel's kingdom, and my magic doesn't work in this cage. It must be something special that he's using."

They ran out of things to say to each other and contemplated their own thoughts. Soon a stack of gold coins moved just slightly. And then the stack of coins disappeared, ever so slowly. Rudy saw this happening and watched until the pile was gone. He looked around and saw another pile starting to move and disappear. He grabbed a coin and pulled. "Agggh!"

They all turned and saw Purloin dangling in the air from a gold coin that he and Rudy were holding. Matinee hurried over and grabbed Purloin. "How did you get here? Did you tunnel under our cage?"

She dropped Purloin at her feet. He bowed and squirmed and said, "I've been following you all the way from the questor's tower. Before you get angry, Tomtee, I am not stealing. Well, maybe borrowing a little gold, but not much."

"Do you know what Snivel will do to you when he finds you?" asked Tomtee. "And why are you here pestering us in the first place?"

"Uh, guys, do you realize he was able to tunnel under the cage. Do you think that is possibly a way out?" asked Josey.

Tomtee and Matina looked to Josey, and then to Purloin who was standing with his hands folded and his face grinning. "Why didn't we think of that?" asked Matina.

Purloin said, "Yes, yes, my tunnel is safe, although it might be tight in certain places."

Billy said, "Tight in certain places! We're four times bigger than you, Purloin. How are we going to fit in there at all?"

Purloin snapped his fingers and dug in his pocket. "I almost forgot—the questor told me to give you these to eat." He held out five green leaves.

"What are they supposed to do?" asked Matina.

Purloin stood proudly. "You will become my size."

"So, if we become your size to go through the tunnel, how do we return to our normal size?" asked Josey.

Scratching his head, Purloin just shrugged his shoulders.

Tomtee quickly took and ate the leaf and immediately was less than two feet tall. "We can worry about that later. Come on, we have to get out of here."

Quickly they all ate the leaves and scrambled toward the tunnel. "Wait!" Tomtee cried. "Purloin, could you get those wooden helmets for us?"

"Go on through the tunnel and I will meet you outside the cavern," said Purloin as he dug a new tunnel so quickly that he had the helmets before they could even leave. Once more they all stood in the gray mist and the smell of rotten eggs surrounded them.

Tomtee snapped his fingers and they were all their normal size.

"Hey, I thought you couldn't use your magic because we were in Snivel's domain," said Josey.

"You're right. Snivel's domain was in the cave, and I was helpless, but now we are in Lusair. He has made this area sick and disgusting, but it is not his domain."

Purloin chimed in, "What do these helmets do? Why are they so light?"

Josey answered him, "They make us invisible—wanna see?" She put the helmet on and disappeared.

Purloin clapped his hands and squealed, "Can I have one? I sure could use it!"

Tomtee glared at him and said, "Definitely not. You would just use it to steal."

Rudy said, "You know, he did rescue us. If it wasn't for him, we'd still be in that cage."

Everyone agreed with Rudy. Tomtee's face become red and grew a mass of frowns, but he finally produced a tiny wooden helmet with a red stone on top for Purloin. "I know I am going to regret this."

Purloin jumped up and kissed Tomtee on the nose.

"Stop that! Now I have a question for you, and I want a truthful answer. Are you following us?"

Purloin hung his head. "I can't tell you."

Tomtee grabbed Purloin and shook him. "You need to tell us why you are following us!"

Finally, he dropped the furlet. Purloin wobbled around, trying to get his balance. He was dizzy and had a hard time walking. "Okay, okay, but you have to promise not to tell the questor. He wanted me to keep an eye on you. It wasn't easy either with you guys fighting monsters; I had to hide all the time and I was constantly scared."

Tomtee was angry and was about to shake Purloin again when Matina grabbed and held Purloin. She talked quietly, thanking the furlet and telling him how brave he was. She slowly put him down when Tomtee had stepped away. "You know Tomtee, he did help us to escape." Quickly she changed everyone into elmorts—even Purloin.

Tomtee glared at her and Purloin. "You know you are breaking the law again, Matina. I hope for your sake we can find your mother. And you, Purloin, I don't know if I believe you, but you did save us, so I guess you can come along."

Purloin wasn't paying attention and instead was inspecting his new body. "Why did you do that? I liked who I was. Whoa! You changed my voice too—it sounds like I'm singing." Then he adopted a low and deep alto, "Tunnel, tunnel, tunnel, we escaped from the tunnel…"

Matina put her hand over Purloin's mouth. "Stop it, Purloin, we don't have time for this. Don't worry—you'll be back to your own self soon. This is our disguise, so Snivel doesn't know what we're saying. We must figure out how to get close to the treasure again without him seeing us."

"Well, I know…"

Josey interrupted Purloin. “Fat chance of that. I only saw one doorway—there were no others.”

“Well, I know…”

“We can’t use the tunnel that brought us out because we’ll just end up in the cage again,” said Tomtee.

Purloin tried again, “If you will let me tell…”

Matina said, “You’re right, but there must be another way in.”

Rudy just stared at Purloin because everyone was ignoring him. He jumped when Purloin finally yelled, “Listen!” He finally got everyone’s attention. “There is another tunnel. When we furlets need to borrow Snivel’s gold we always burrow two tunnels—one in and another out, just in case we need it. But you will have to take off your shoes and be as quiet as a butterfly sailing on the wind.”

“Put on your helmets before we go into the tunnel, and don’t take them off for anything,” Tomtee instructed.

“You guys are forgetting something,” Josey said.

Matina was impatient to get back inside and find her mother. “What part were you not paying attention to?” Matina growled.

Josey put her hands on her hips and narrowed her eyes. “I did not miss anything and listened to everything, but you are forgetting something. We are not small anymore. We’re our normal size.”

Matina burst into tears, "I'm so sorry, but if you look you will see the moons are going to meet any minute now and we need to get in there."

Tomtee instantly made them smaller. "We still have time, Matina. Josey, you have been paying attention for a long time now. Good thinking about our size. Okay, now no speaking—you don't know what good ears Snivel has."

Purloin lead them to a rock that was near the cave. He pushed the rock aside and jumped down. The others followed. It was a tight squeeze, but they were able to crawl and use their headband moonlights to see where they were going. Purloin stopped and so did they. He could feel Snivel come back into the cave, searching. They waited a long time. Josey's leg was cramping when finally Purloin started moving again. Purloin came to a place in the mountain of jewelry that had a large indentation and carefully poked his head up through the jewels. He made sure his hat was on and slowly raised his head and looked around—it was all clear. The others followed him out of the tunnel, securing their hats as they moved, and crawled over to a cave made entirely of gold bricks.

Matina whispered, "Josey, do you see anything that might give us a clue about my mother?"

"Me? I don't even know what to look for. If I'm supposed to be the one to find her, I wish I knew how. There must be millions of jewels here."

Tomtee moved out of the cave and stood on a huge gold brick with a gold shovel. “We could dig here forever and never find the right jewel. Uh-oh, here comes Snivel.”

They ran back to the gold cave to hide and watched Snivel as he flew slowly over them. Landing on the other side of the mounds of gold he said, “They got away. I can’t leave to find them for there is not enough time. Soon, soon, so very soon.” In a raspy voice that trembled he kept repeating, “THE TIME WILL BE SOON. PINK-SPINEL, EMERALDS, AMETHYST, RUBIES, AND LAPIS.”

They all sat quietly, listening. At times, the Snivel’s eyes watered close to tears. “Amethyst, rubies, no, pink-spinel, rubies. . . no, no,” he blustered. He chanted the jewels’ names time and time again. “Pink-spinel, emeralds, amethyst, rubies, and lapis-luzili.” Always in the same order, except when he managed to confuse himself. Josey and the others sat quietly and listened. In a fit of anger, Snivel flew away.

“Why was he saying the names of those jewels over and over?” Cully asked.

“Maybe it’s a clue of some kind,” Matina said.

“Maybe it’s a code. In school we’ve been learning about codes and how to make them. Why don’t we take the first letter of each word and see if it spells anything? If that doesn’t work, then we can take the last letter,” Josey whispered.

Tomtee joined in, “He started with pink-spinel, then emerald, amethyst, rubies, and lapis.”

Suddenly Josey knew. “Psearl? No, it’s pearl!” She looked around and saw a large pearl perched on top a mountain of gold. “Look! That must be your mother.”

They all gazed at a large pearl that had a brilliant luster and glow about it. “It's just an illusion—no pearl is that big,” Matina sighed.

Cully pulled a large eyeglass out of his pocket and looked at the pearl. “But it’s not! That pearl is your mother. The questor knew you wouldn’t be able to see through illusions in Snivel’s cave, so he gave me this spy glass.”

“Let me see,” Tomtee said as he grabbed the spy glass. “Matina, it is your mother.”

“What should we do now?” Josey asked.

“First, we become beetles, so we can crawl as close as we can to the pearl. Then I will change us into birds, so then we can fly the rest of the way…”

Cully and Billy said together, “Why didn’t you do that before?”

Matina hissed in a whisper, “Because the cage stopped my powers just like it did for Tomtee. Put your helmets away so we can use them later.”

Purloin quickly tucked his helmet in his pants so that Tomtee couldn’t take it.

Snivel entered the cavern on the other side of the mountain of jewels. His sad song echoed as the five beetles scurried up the mountain of treasure before they instantly turned into five white doves that flew up to the huge pearl.

As the white doves came close to the white pearl, they were caught once again. Snivel swooped in with the gold cage turned upside down and scooped them all in it. He plopped them down roughly, next to the large white pearl.

"No!" screamed Matina. "Let my mother go!"

CHAPTER 10

"HA! YOU'VE ESCAPED FROM YOUR GOLDEN CELL. WELL, AS YOU CAN SEE, YOU ARE BACK IN IT. I SEE YOU'VE EVEN FIGURED OUT WHERE THE QUEEN IS. IT DOES YOU NO GOOD," shouted Snivel.

Matina stamped her foot. "Let my mother go!"

Snivel laughed, "YOUR MOTHER? YOU WANT YOUR MOTHER!" He rocked back and forth on his heels and mocked Matina. "BABY, BABY, BABY! BABY WANTS HER MOTHER!"

In a deep menacing voice he said, "The moons are touching, and it won't be long now."

Matina tried to reach out to her mother, but the rungs were too close together. Josey and Rudy grabbed one rung and Billy and Tomtee grabbed the one next to it and they pulled with all their might. Finally, the rungs moved ever so slightly—just enough so that Matina was able to put her arm through and at least touch her mother. As soon as she touched her mother's feet, Snivel started reciting his spell but got confused and had to start over.

Matina stretched her arms though the bars of the golden cage, tears streaming down her face. The ring on her finger began to glow, forming a large circle of light. She saw her mother's feet and looked up into her mother's smiling face. Behind her stood the Knight of Light.

"Matina, do you remember what the questor told you to do?" Cully whispered.

She looked at her hand and saw the ring glowing in a circle of light. Matina quickly took the ring off her finger and placed it on her mother's finger. A shower of sparkling lights encircled the group.

They heard Snivel scream, "NO! IT CANNOT BE! SO CLOSE! NO, NO. . ." His voice faded as they rose through the circle of lights.

Lights exploded over the questor's tower then spilled through the roof and settled onto the floor. The lights faded away, leaving Josey and her friends in the questor's tower. It was cold and dark; sunshine did not shine through the walls. Everyone was puzzled because the questor's tower always had sun shining through the walls.

"Master, Master," Cully called as he ran up the circular stairs.

Tomtee looked around at the room; books were everywhere, but that was normal. He looked at the desk and everything was in disarray, but that was how the questor worked.

Cully came back up the stairs. "The questor was not in the tower."

"Maybe someone needed him," Tomtee said.

"No. Something has happened to him," Cully said. "The tower has never been like this before, even when he was gone. There has always been light here and never, never has it been so dark."

The queen and Matina stood embracing, not saying a word as the others discussed what could have happened to the questor.

Matina noticed her mother and asked her if anything was wrong. Instead of joyful relief there was a look of concern on her face. She slowly turned toward the group. "YOU THINK YOU ARE SO SMART. I MAY NOT HAVE THE QUEEN, BUT THE QUESTOR IS NOW MY PRISONER. MY TIME GROWS SHORT, BUT UNLESS YOU GIVE ME THE QUEEN, HE WILL SURELY DIE."

Without warning the queen collapsed on the floor. They all rushed to help her and lifted her to a chair. "I don't know how Snivel did it, but he has Lucas. We need to rescue him—he is being tortured. We need to go see your grandmother, Matina."

The queen revived and knew what to do. She waived her hand, and they entered Grandmother's room, all hurrying through. Grandmother was not at all pleased that Matina had put herself and her friends in danger. After chiding her, she questioned Cully because he was the closest to the questor.

The queen sat on her mother's bed and said, "We must contact the Knight of Light, for only he can help the questor."

Cully wasn't sure how to contact the Knight of Light, but he remembered how the questor stood at night on top of the tower.

Clearing his voice he said, "There is a balcony area on top of the tower, and when the questor was troubled or needed answers, he went up there. When he came back, he was refreshed and had all his answers. What he did up there I don't know, but that could be how he contacted the Knight of Light."

"Then let's try it," said Matina.

Tomtee and the others agreed and wanted to start right away.

A small voice coming from under Grandmother's bed said, "It sounds too easy."

"Come out from under my bed, Purloin," commanded Grandmother.

He immediately came out and stood on the end of the bed. "I didn't jump on your bed…"

"Of course you didn't. I put you there. Now tell us, why do you think it is too easy?"

Purloin squirmed and bowed his head. "I used to sneak up to the balcony when the questor wasn't looking. He would just sit there and watch the setting sun or the rising moon. He didn't do anything special. It was peaceful and even I felt good afterward, but I didn't see the Knight of Light—I just saw the sun or moon rays."

The room was quiet a long time. Grandmother asked, "Purloin, when you were up there could you see the sun or moon? You just said all you saw were the rays of the sun or moon."

Purloin lifted his head and said, "No. No, I didn't see the sun or moon or even the questor. I was behind a tall square box. I could hear him talking but didn't dare peek to see if he was just talking to himself or someone else. So maybe he was talking to the Knight of Light."

Tomtee scowled at the furlet and said, "It would be worth going to try. If it doesn't work at least we'd be at the tower, and we can look in his workroom to see if we can find any clues."

~ ~ ~

The group was ready to head out to the tower. The queen told them that she would assist by looking in the Books of

Wisdom to see if she could find out how to contact the Knight of Light. It would take many days as there were so many books. She asked if they were ready and then transported them to the tower.

"Wow, this is a lot easier than walking!!" Josey exclaimed.

"Cully, how do we get to the balcony?" Tomtee asked.

"I don't know."

Tomtee couldn't believe it. "What do you mean you don't know? You have lived here all these years and you don't know?"

"I was always trying to straighten the workshop up in the evening…"

Everyone turned and looked at Purloin. "Well, you know the picture of the queen next to the window. All you have to do is lift the right corner up just a little and put it back down again."

Tomtee wasn't sure he believed Purloin, but they climbed the steps to the top of the tower. He marched over to the picture and did as Purloin said. A door slid open with steps leading upward. They all followed Tomtee up on the balcony and saw a beautiful view of the country going from deserts to valleys to beautiful hillsides.

"Why is everything here so beautiful and outside of this land everything is dying?" asked Josey.

"Because this is the questor's land that has not been touched by the evil; his power is too strong," answered Cully.

Rudy looked around and saw the tall square box where Purloin was hiding behind. And behind the box there was a scroll with dates on it. “What does this scroll say?”

Cully answered, “It says, ‘This tower is a Guardian—a sentinel for troubled times. He who seeks truth, it will be given to him. He who seeks knowledge, it will be shown to him. He who seeks wisdom will find it.’”

“That is all well and good, but doesn’t it tell us how to get all that truth, knowledge, and wisdom?” said Josey.

No one answered because no one knew the answer. They sat on the marble bench and looked out at the slowly sinking sun. Nothing was happening. Purloin went to his usual spot and waited. Nothing stirred, no birds were singing, no wind blowing. Just as the last ray was glowing, a bright light enveloped it and grew larger.

“It must be the Knight of Light,” Matina said softly.

Purloin scurried out to the marble bench and sat next to Matina’s feet.

A large man covered in armor and boots made of bronze gleamed in the sunlight as he sat on a huge white horse. The gold on his belt caught a ray of sun that split the light. He took off his helmet, revealing eyes like flames and snow-white hair falling to his shoulders. His voice was like deep thunder. “I see Purloin helped lead you here. You don’t need my help. You defeated Snivel once and you can do it again. You all have special talents and strengths—you just have to use them.”

"Does the scroll help us to find the answers?" asked Tomtee.

"You can find the answers within yourselves. You also can use your gift to find the answers in the questor's workshop. The only thing I will tell you is this: when you confront Snivel, link your hands, for the light within you will destroy him. You all have a strong light within yourselves."

Slowly the circle of light began to disappear. Rudy yelled, "But where are the answers to the scroll?"

"In the questor's workshop. . ."

Once the Knight of Light disappeared it was dark. Matina used her fire to light the torches on the wall. No one said anything at first because they felt full of hope and excited to try and find the answers. It took a moment for them to recover from seeing the Knight of Light. Once they regrouped, Matina led them down the stairs, lighting torches until they came to the questor's workshop. Upon arriving they couldn't decide where to start. There were so many books.

Rudy started shuffling through books and found one that said *Truth*. He opened it and came across a passage, "The elmorts must admit to the people that they failed to watch out for them. They failed to be honest and truthful, and their greed took over and allowed Snivel to ruin the land and spread his evil," it read.

"Matina, I may have found something, but I don't think you are going to like it," Rudy cautioned.

Matina took the book and read the passage. She put her head down and began shaking it back and forth. "I need to go show this to Mother. She needs to go before the people and let them know. That is the only way we are going to get this evil to release its hold."

Matina disappeared and reappeared quickly. "How did you do that, Matina?" Purloin asked.

"Mother gave me her ring and showed me how to be in different places in a flash. She is taking the book to the castle leaders and will make the announcement to all the people of Lusair within the hour."

Josey kept thinking of the scroll and concentrated on the line: *If you want knowledge, it will be shown to you.* She saw the questor's telescope. *Hmm, maybe that will show me something,* she thought. She gasped at what she saw. Quickly she called Matina and the others to look. Far away in Snivel's cave, they saw the questor. He was black and blue and bloodied.

Snivel took his fury out on the questor. "You're nothing! I will drain your power until you end up being a sniveling magician with no real powers. How dare you send mere mortals against me!"

The questor thought to himself that it was odd being beaten and pummeled by an invisible thing. He couldn't defend himself, for he never knew from when or where a blow might come. Through his bleeding swollen lips he replied, "They may be mere mortals, but they defeated you."

Something grabbed and pulled a clump of hairs from the questor's beard, leaving a bloodied jaw. "NOT FOR LONG! We will see just how valuable and strong you are. You cannot stand against me."

Using a different tactic, the questor asked, "Why would you want the queen? She is no good to you now, the moons have already passed over each other. Besides, your time is at an end, you don't have long now to live."

"DON'T YOU THINK I KNOW THAT. I ALMOST DEPLETED MY POWER TAKING YOU. AT LEAST THE CAVE CAN HELP ME TO GAIN SOME POWER." He leaned on a pile of gold and stared at the questor. Soon there were snores.

The questor knew Snivel was near the end and everything he did was an effort. He thought, *I can hear his snores, he must be sleeping. How foolish of me to let my guard down.*

Back at the tower, Cully wept and paced the room after seeing how the questor looked in the telescope. He went about looking for more clues. The small group was subdued, frantically trying to find answers on how to rescue him. Eventually, they sat down and talked about what they knew so far. The first step was completed when the elmorts admitted their guilt in not governing the land and allowing the Snivel to do what he wanted. They also found out he was weak and dying.

"What did it mean his cavern was recharging him?" asked Billy.

Tomtee was reading through some papers and said, "According to these notes that the questor wrote about Snivel—he is dying, and his power will become weaker. The recharging of himself by the cavern is just to allow him to breathe and move and will not replenish his powers to full strength."

"It must have taken a lot of his powers to capture the questor, and he has no way to replenish them fully, right?" asked Purloin.

They all stopped and stared at Purloin. "What?" Scratching some dirt out of his ear he continued, "He must be very weak by now. Think about it. To capture the questor probably took all his strength so he must be weak now. We need to attack now."

Matina and Tomtee shook their heads. "Sounds like a great idea," Rudy and Josey exclaimed together.

Matina said, "Tomtee and I agree, we're just surprised that Purloin was the one to come up with the idea. Now we need a plan. Suggestions, anyone?"

Josey got up and started pacing. "Snivel is very weak by now because he couldn't use the queen for her strength. We know from the books what had to be done before we attempted a rescue, and the queen is informing the people of her failure. The telescope gave us knowledge of where the questor is and how he is being tortured. It also showed how weak Snivel is."

"Tomtee and Matina, you have to use your powers to get the questor out before Snivel is strong again. Does your mother have another ring so that Tomtee could travel quickly with you to the cave?"

Rudy couldn't believe how Josey had been listening throughout all the things that had happened and came up with the beginnings of a plan.

Instantly Matina disappeared and then reappeared, excited and disappointed at the same time. Excited the questor would be saved, but disappointed because they could not help in the rescue. They needed to be wise and let Mother and Grandmother bring the questor home so that the scroll could be fulfilled.

Before Matina finished talking, the questor was standing before them—dirty, bruised, half his beard missing, smelling like smoke—but smiling. "Thank you for helping the queen to set me free."

Cully and Purloin rushed over, hugging the questor and pushing him into a chair. Smiling, he waited until they were through. "All of you are champions of Lusair."

"Well, I guess we are done here," Josey said.

"Time to hit the road," Billy agreed.

Purloin rushed up to Rudy and said, "Hitting the road? What did it do to you?"

"No, no, it's just an expression," Rudy replied.

Purloin said his goodbyes, put on his wooden helmet, and disappeared.

Tomtee said, "We will regret the day he earned that helmet."

Everyone laughed and gathered around the questor. There were hugs all around and the questor finally opened a window of time and Josey, Billy, and Rudy ran through.

Rudy waved goodbye to Josey as she climbed back into her bedroom and ran into the kitchen.

"Mom, you'll never believe what happened!"

"I'm sorry dear, but I don't have time to listen right now—maybe later. We have unexpected company coming for dinner and I need you to go to the store. Grab a paper and pencil and make a list of things I need."

"I don't need to write it down, just tell me what you need."

Josey's mother looked at her, "Do you feel okay?"

Josey smiled and thought, *I never knew Mom had such a pearly glow to her hair*. Finally, she said, "Trust me!"

"If you don't bring back what I need, you'll have to run back again," Mother warned, as she listed six items she needed from the store. Josey ran all the way to the market and back, returning with all the items her mother wanted.

"Josey, this is wonderful. You really did listen. While I fix dinner, please go and clean your room before our company arrives."

"Okay, Mom."

Josey cleaned her room and wondered if she had been dreaming about her adventures. *I have to ask Rudy—he was there.* She hoped it was real. Sighing, she bent over to pick up her shoe from under the bed and found a necklace with a large pearl.

“I wasn't dreaming!” she laughed.

About the Author
Sharon Leino

The oldest girl in a family of 11, Sharon always had a great imagination. As a child, she expressed herself through poetry, pouring out her feelings about love, adventure, anger, and being bullied. When her father died, she quit writing and threw away all her poetry. She's asked herself why, but just decided that, "Sometimes we do some dumb things in our lives."

As a grownup, Sharon's career as an educator and special education curriculum developer found her writing reports and grants. She kept extensive journals of her travels with her beloved husband to the many countries and states they visited.

Her childhood love of writing resurfaced with a vengeance when she retired and became a Texas snowbird. After joining various writer's groups, it became clear she had a passion for writing inspiring books for children. Just as this happened, her husband lost his sight, and her stories were packed away to make room for their new adventure that was full of trials but also love and joy. Florida became their home where Sharon still lives, making a new life for herself on her own. Her days are full of volunteering at church, creating jewelry as an amateur silversmith, and of course, writing.

www.sharonleinoauthor.com

Also from Author Sharon Leino:

Ten-year-old Rudy is afraid of everything, and to top it off, two bullies like to chase him home from school! Every day those bullies try to make Rudy do things he's scared to do. Rudy's best friend Billy is usually there to defend him, but some days Billy is at Taekwondo class, and when that happens, Rudy finds himself panicked with fear.

One day Billy convinces Rudy to go fishing with him at a pond deep in the forest. What was meant to be a fun time together becomes the scariest experience of their lives. Rudy, trembling with fear and worry at every turn, mysteriously finds himself and his best friend lost in a strange world full of danger.

In *Scaredy, Book 1 of the Adventures in Lusair*, Rudy must learn to conquer his fears and find his power. The life of his best friend and the fate of this strange new world depends on it.

Available on Amazon & wherever books are sold.

Made in the USA
Columbia, SC
12 April 2023